Tides Of Deception

Michael Ferguson

Published by Michael Ferguson, 2024.

TIDES OF DECEPTION

First edition. September 17, 2024.

ISBN: 979-8227528957

Written by Michael Ferguson.

Chapter 1: The Calm Before the Storm

Jack Kincaid sat on the edge of a rocky bluff, staring out at the endless stretch of the Pacific Ocean. The wind tugged at his graying hair, and the briny scent of saltwater filled his lungs. His old fishing boat bobbed gently in the distance, tied to the makeshift dock he'd built from weathered driftwood. This had been his life for the past two years—a life of isolation, far removed from the man he used to be.

He didn't mind the solitude. Out here, there was no noise. No headlines. No missions. No reminders of his failures. The island, a small, uncharted speck in the Pacific, had been his refuge since the world had gone to hell. For Jack, it was a place to forget.

The mornings were quiet, the afternoons long, and the nights bitterly cold. But Jack welcomed the cold. It was the only thing that could keep him numb, to suppress the memories that clawed at the edges of his mind when he let his guard down. He had stopped caring about the things that used to matter: honor, duty, camaraderie. All that had died the day he failed.

He got up from the bluff and made his way down the uneven path toward his cabin. The small wooden structure was as rugged as the man who lived in it—barely more than a single room with a bed, a stove, and a few sparse pieces of furniture. It was enough. Jack didn't need much, and he liked it that way.

The nightmares, though—they didn't care about simplicity or solitude. They found him every night, bringing him back to that day in Afghanistan when everything had gone wrong. The mission, a joint operation with local forces, had been simple: extract hostages from a terrorist compound and get out clean. But it hadn't gone that way. Not even close.

The village had been full of civilians. Jack and his team moved in, and before they could react, a child—a little girl with wide, innocent eyes—had run toward them. A split second later, the world exploded in fire and debris. The girl had been wired with explosives. The hostages, the civilians, Jack's teammates—all gone in an instant.

Jack survived, but barely. The physical wounds healed over time, but the guilt never left. The little girl's face haunted him, a constant reminder of what he had failed to stop. He tried to bury it deep, telling himself that he had no control over it. But the military wasn't as forgiving. Someone had to take the fall, and that someone had been Jack Kincaid.

They called it negligence. He called it betrayal. His superiors had turned their backs on him, washing their hands of the blood spilled in that village. It wasn't just a failed mission—it was the end of everything he had ever known. They stripped him of his rank, dishonorably discharged him, and left him to rot.

Jack didn't fight it. After the investigation, he'd simply walked away. He bought an old boat with what little savings he had left and sailed until he found this island. And he hadn't looked back since.

Inside the cabin, he opened the door to a modest shelf filled with supplies: canned beans, dried fish, and some stale crackers he had traded for at a distant fishing village months ago. Jack sat down at the rough-hewn table, pushing the thoughts away as he prepared to eat. He wasn't one for rituals, but this one had become routine—keep busy, keep moving, and don't let the memories win.

The wind howled outside, a prelude to an incoming storm. Jack glanced at the horizon. Dark clouds gathered in the distance, churning like the tempest that constantly roiled inside him. A storm wasn't unusual this time of year. The Pacific had a way of reminding you who was in charge, and Jack had learned to respect its temper. He bolted the windows and checked the locks on the doors. There wasn't much to protect, but the howling wind would turn into driving rain soon enough.

As the storm grew closer, he heard the low rumble of thunder and the steady crash of waves against the rocky shore. He leaned back in his chair, staring at the flickering flame of the lantern on the table. For a brief moment, he felt the weight of his past loosen its grip, lulled by the rhythmic pulse of the storm.

Then a distant noise snapped him back to reality—a sound that didn't belong. Jack's head tilted, his body tensing instinctively. It was faint, but unmistakable: the high-pitched whine of an engine.

No one came to this island. Not fishermen, not tourists, not anyone. The only boat out there was his, and it was tied securely to the dock. Jack stood up, eyes narrowing as he moved toward the door.

The storm had fully arrived, rain now lashing against the cabin with ferocity. Jack grabbed a weathered jacket, pulling it on as he stepped outside into the howling wind. The rain stung his face, but he ignored it, focusing on the direction of the sound. It was getting closer—an engine, small but persistent, cutting through the noise of the storm.

He moved down the path toward the beach, his eyes scanning the dark, rolling waves. Lightning flashed, illuminating the churning sea for a brief moment. That's when he saw it: a small boat, barely holding together, drifting toward the shore. Jack's instincts flared, the years of training kicking in despite the isolation. Something was wrong.

As the boat came closer, he could make out the outline of figures inside—people. Too many people for such a small vessel, and none of them seemed to be in control of it. The boat was at the mercy of the storm, tossed about like a toy. Jack's pulse quickened, the isolation that had been his solace suddenly shattered.

When the boat finally hit the shore, it didn't land softly. It crashed into the rocks with a sickening crunch, throwing several figures into the freezing water. Jack rushed forward, his boots sinking into the wet sand as he reached the shoreline.

"Help!" a voice screamed. A woman's voice, faint but desperate. Jack didn't hesitate. He plunged into the icy water, his powerful arms cutting through the waves as he reached the wreckage.

There were bodies in the water—alive, but barely. He grabbed the nearest person, a young woman, and pulled her to the shore. She was coughing, gasping for air, her face pale from cold and fear. Jack didn't stop to ask questions. He waded back into the surf, pulling another woman to safety, then another.

When the last of them was on the beach, Jack stepped back, breathing heavily. His mind raced as he took in the scene—six women, all soaked, bruised, and terrified. They huddled together on the sand, eyes wide with fear, as the rain poured down in sheets.

"What happened?" Jack demanded, his voice sharp.

One of the women, older than the rest and with a deep gash on her forehead, looked up at him with haunted eyes. "We escaped," she said, her voice trembling. "They were going to kill us."

Jack's blood ran cold. "Who?"

She swallowed hard, her gaze darting to the wrecked boat as if the answer lay in the shattered hull. "The Colonel," she whispered. "He's using this island."

Jack felt his stomach twist. He hadn't heard that name in years, not since the mission—the one that had ruined him. The Colonel had been his commanding officer, the man who had orchestrated the operation that went so disastrously wrong. The man who had betrayed him.

The world tilted slightly, a rush of adrenaline surging through Jack's veins as he processed what he had just heard. His island wasn't just a quiet refuge anymore—it was a battleground. And The Colonel, the man he thought he'd left behind with the rest of his past, was back.

This time, though, it wasn't just Jack's life on the line. The storm wasn't just a force of nature—it was the harbinger of something far more dangerous.

Jack Kincaid awoke to the sound of crashing waves, louder than usual, pounding relentlessly against the rocky shore. He rolled off the rough mattress he called a bed and stretched, shaking off the last remnants of sleep. His small cabin was silent, save for the distant roar of the Pacific. The storm had blown through during the night, leaving a trail of debris along the coastline, and the air was thick with the briny smell of the ocean. Jack liked it this way—no one to bother him, no demands to pull him away from his exile.

He stepped outside into the cool morning air, taking in the sight of the island. The sky was still heavy with the aftermath of the storm, dark clouds clinging stubbornly to the horizon. The island was remote, small, and covered in dense, unruly vegetation that had been battered by the wind and rain. Jack had chosen it for its isolation, a place where he could disappear and avoid the world that had done him wrong.

But as he gazed out across the beach, something was different. Something caught his eye—movement where there shouldn't have been any. His instincts, long dormant but never entirely extinguished, flared to life. He squinted, his eyes tracing the shoreline until they landed on a cluster of dark shapes, barely distinguishable against the wet sand.

People.

At first, Jack thought it might have been debris washed ashore, the remnants of a wrecked boat or cargo scattered by the storm. But as he moved closer, the shapes took form, and a sickening realization hit him like a punch to the gut. These weren't lifeless objects—they were bodies.

His pace quickened as he trudged through the thick sand, boots sinking with each step. Jack reached the first figure, a woman, her face pale and lips blue from the cold. He knelt beside her, his heart pounding in his chest. She was alive, but just barely. Her breath came in shallow, irregular gasps, and her skin was cold to the touch.

Jack's mind raced, a mix of adrenaline and instinct. This was no ordinary shipwreck. He looked further down the beach and saw more women, scattered like driftwood, their bodies battered by the storm. They were dressed in rags, some barefoot, and all looked as though they had been through hell.

He counted five in total, all alive but in desperate condition. Jack's hands tightened into fists as he scanned the horizon, searching for signs of whatever vessel had brought them here. But there was nothing—no wreckage, no sign of a boat. It was as if they had materialized out of the storm itself.

"Who are you?" Jack muttered under his breath, but he knew they wouldn't be able to answer. At least, not yet.

Without wasting time, Jack scooped up the woman closest to him. She was light, too light, her body frail and weak. He carried her back toward the cabin, his mind working through a thousand possibilities, none of them good. Whoever these women were, they weren't tourists, and they hadn't come here by choice.

As he reached the cabin, Jack gently laid the woman down on the small, worn couch inside. He went to work quickly, lighting a fire in the stone hearth to warm the space. The storm had dropped the temperature, and these women wouldn't survive much longer without heat. He moved back outside, retrieving the others one by one, placing them near the fire to dry and warm up.

The room felt cramped now, the bodies of the survivors strewn about like casualties of some forgotten war. Jack wiped sweat from his brow and checked each one for signs of life. They were all breathing, albeit weakly, and for that, he was grateful. But their condition was dire, and if he didn't act soon, some of them wouldn't make it through the day.

He grabbed a jug of water from the small wooden shelf in the corner and began carefully pouring it into each of their mouths, hoping to hydrate them. As he worked, Jack's mind spun back to his days in the Navy SEALs. He had been trained for high-pressure situations, for saving lives in the worst of conditions. But it had been a long time since those skills had been tested.

One of the women stirred. Her eyelids fluttered, and she let out a soft moan. Jack knelt beside her, placing a steadying hand on her shoulder.

"Hey, you're safe now," he said softly. "You're going to be okay."

Her eyes opened, wide with fear, darting around the room as if she were still trapped in whatever nightmare had brought her here. She tried to speak, but her voice cracked, barely more than a whisper.

"Water..." she rasped.

Jack helped her take another sip. She drank slowly, her body shaking with every movement.

"What happened?" he asked, keeping his voice calm, though inside, his nerves were frayed.

She swallowed, her throat working hard to get the words out. "They... they took us... forced us..."

"Who did?" Jack pressed.

Her gaze met his, and Jack saw a deep, unyielding terror in her eyes. "Men. Bad men. They... they're on the island."

Jack felt a chill that had nothing to do with the cold. He leaned back, processing her words. Traffickers. It had to be. The signs were all there—women taken against their will, washed ashore after a storm, no wreckage to be found. Whoever had brought them here was still out there, likely using the island as a base.

"How many?" Jack asked, his voice dropping to a near growl.

"I don't know," she whispered. "More than... more than I could count. They kept us in the dark. Locked away. We thought we'd never escape."

Jack felt a surge of anger rising in his chest, but he forced it down. Now wasn't the time to lose control. These women needed him focused, not enraged.

"Stay here," he said, standing up and heading toward the door. "I'm going to check the perimeter. I'll be back."

She grabbed his arm, her fingers cold and weak, but her grip was firm. "Don't go out there. They'll kill you."

Jack gave her a hard look. "They'll have to try."

Outside, the wind had picked up again, and the waves were crashing violently against the shore. Jack scanned the horizon, searching for any signs of movement. The island was deceptively quiet, the kind of silence that only followed something catastrophic. But Jack knew better than to trust it. His instincts were screaming that this wasn't over.

He moved along the beach, his boots sinking into the wet sand, eyes alert for any sign of the traffickers. If they were using the island as a base, they would be nearby, probably hidden somewhere deeper inland. Jack's mind raced, piecing together a plan. He couldn't take on an unknown number of men alone—not without more information, more intel. But he could start by scouting the area, gathering whatever clues he could find.

The woman's words echoed in his mind: More than I could count.

He found tracks in the sand, faint but visible. Boot prints, leading from the water toward the thick underbrush. Jack knelt beside them, his heart pounding in his chest. They were fresh—too fresh. Whoever had been here was still close by.

Jack stood, his jaw clenched. His past had taught him to be methodical, to never rush into a situation without knowing exactly what he was up against. But this was different. These traffickers had brought their filth to his island, and they had to be stopped.

A distant noise caught his attention—voices, low and indistinct, carried on the wind. Jack turned toward the sound, his hand instinctively moving to the knife strapped to his belt. He crept forward, slipping into the underbrush, moving silently through the dense foliage.

The voices grew clearer, though still muffled by the rustling leaves and the distant roar of the ocean. Jack could hear at least two men talking, their words angry and sharp. He moved closer, carefully parting the bushes until he could see the source of the voices.

Two men stood near a small boat, arguing in harsh tones. Both were armed, rifles slung over their shoulders, their clothes dirty and worn. Jack recognized the type—mercenaries, hired muscle. They were distracted, caught up in their argument, and hadn't noticed him.

Jack's pulse quickened. He had to make a choice: confront them now and risk alerting the rest of the group, or fall back, gather more information, and strike when the odds were in his favor.

His SEAL training kicked in—calculated risk was part of the job. Jack silently retreated, moving back through the underbrush and toward the cabin. He needed to regroup, plan his next move. He couldn't rush this, not if he wanted to get these women off the island alive.

When he returned to the cabin, the women were still huddled near the fire, their eyes wide with fear. Jack knew they were counting on him, trusting him to protect them from whatever horrors awaited outside.

He knelt beside the woman who had spoken earlier. "There are men out there. Armed. Do you know how many?"

She shook her head. "We never saw them all. They kept us in the dark. But... there's more. It's not just us."

Jack frowned. "What do you mean?"

"They're using this place," she said, her voice trembling. "For more than just us. Weapons. Drugs. I heard them talking. They said something about a shipment... something big. They're expecting more men."

Jack's stomach tightened. This was bigger than he had thought. Much bigger.

He stood, his resolve hardening. He had to act fast, before things spiraled even further out of control.

"Stay here," he said, grabbing his gear. "I'm going to stop them."

As he stepped outside once more, the storm clouds began to gather again, darkening the sky. Jack knew that time was running out—for him, for the women, and for whatever dark forces were about to converge on the island.

Chapter 2: Stirring the Waters

Jack Kincaid sat at the edge of his weathered porch, staring out at the endless expanse of ocean. His mind was a whirlwind of conflicting thoughts, none of which provided any comfort. The women he had found washed ashore were huddled together inside the small cabin, murmuring in their native tongue. Fear still clung to them, like the damp chill that permeated the island air after the storm.

He clenched his jaw and rubbed the back of his neck, the tension building with each passing second. Every instinct told him to walk away, to leave this mess to someone else—someone better suited to deal with it. He had left the world of violence behind, or at least, he had tried. But now, fate had a cruel way of dragging him back in.

"Just my luck," he muttered under his breath.

Jack's mind raced back to the conversation with Maria, the woman who had taken charge of the group of survivors. She was strong, her English good enough to convey the horrors they'd endured. The bruises on her arms and the haunted look in her eyes told him everything he needed to know, even before she spoke.

"They'll come for us," she had said, her voice low and firm. "They always come."

Jack had felt the cold weight of her words. He wasn't naive; he knew the world was filled with darkness, and men like the ones she described thrived in the shadows. Trafficking, drugs, weapons—it was the kind of evil that festered in places far removed from the public eye, and now, it seemed, that evil had found its way to his doorstep.

For the past few years, Jack had done everything in his power to avoid involvement in anything resembling a mission. He had retired, exiled himself to this remote island to escape the nightmares of his past. But now, he was faced with a choice he didn't want to make. The women inside were depending on him, but the weight of responsibility pressed down on him like an anchor.

He shook his head, trying to dispel the thoughts that kept creeping into his mind. I'm no hero, he reminded himself. He had failed before—failed spectacularly. And innocent people had paid the price.

A gust of wind swept in from the ocean, carrying with it the salty tang of the sea and the sound of distant thunder. The storm hadn't entirely passed, and Jack knew the calm would only be temporary. Just like this situation.

Maria's words echoed in his mind again. They always come.

Jack felt the familiar stir of adrenaline building in his gut, a sensation he hadn't felt in years. It was the same feeling he had before every mission—before everything went wrong. His instincts were telling him to gear up, to prepare for a fight, but his heart wanted no part of it.

The memory of that day, the failed mission, slammed into him like a wave. The cries of the civilians, the explosion that tore through the village, the sickening realization that he had been betrayed. Jack had carried the weight of that moment ever since, using the isolation of this island as a way to escape his guilt. But now, here he was, standing on the edge of a decision he didn't want to make.

He stood up abruptly, pacing along the edge of the porch. He couldn't think like this. He needed clarity, and the best way to get that was through action. Jack grabbed his rifle from inside the cabin, checking the scope and the rounds in the magazine with practiced efficiency. The familiarity of the motion brought a strange sense of calm, a muscle memory that reminded him of who he used to be.

But then the faces of the women, their fear, crept back into his mind.

He couldn't just ignore them.

Jack slammed the magazine into the rifle and set it aside. He took a deep breath, trying to steady the torrent of emotions raging inside him. He needed to clear his head, and the best way to do that was by taking a walk. The island wasn't big, but it had enough hidden coves and rocky cliffs that could conceal something—or someone. If what Maria had said was true, the smuggling operation had been using this island as a hidden base. That meant there could be more signs of their presence nearby.

Grabbing his weathered leather jacket, Jack stepped off the porch, the crunch of gravel under his boots grounding him as he made his way toward the dense tree line. The island was his refuge, his sanctuary, and he knew every inch of it. If there were any clues to be found, he'd find them.

As he walked, Jack's mind drifted back to his time in the SEALs. Back then, the world was black and white—there were enemies, and there were allies. You followed orders, you completed the mission, and you trusted your team. But all of that had been stripped away from him in one single, devastating moment. Now, everything was gray, and trust was a luxury he no longer had.

The path narrowed as Jack moved deeper into the forest, the trees growing thicker around him. His senses sharpened, scanning for any signs of disturbance—broken branches, fresh tracks, anything that might indicate someone else had been here recently. The island was usually quiet, save for the occasional wildlife and the ever-present sound of the waves crashing against the cliffs.

But now, there was an undercurrent of tension in the air, like the island itself was holding its breath.

Jack pushed through the thick brush, his gaze sweeping the area for anything out of place. He moved with the same silent precision he had been trained to use in the field, every step deliberate, every breath controlled. It wasn't long before he found the first sign: a series of deep tire tracks in the soft earth. They were fresh, likely made in the last 24 hours.

He crouched down, running his fingers along the edge of the track. The pattern was unmistakable—military-grade vehicles. Whoever was running this operation, they had resources. That wasn't a surprise, but it confirmed his worst fear: this wasn't just some small-time smuggling ring. This was organized, efficient, and well-funded.

Jack followed the tracks deeper into the forest, his pulse quickening. The further he went, the more disturbed the ground became. There were signs of foot traffic—multiple people, all moving in the same direction. He scanned the area, noticing a faint trail of broken branches leading off the main path.

The smell of burning wood reached him before he saw the smoke. Jack slowed his pace, his hand instinctively going to the knife strapped to his thigh. He moved cautiously, staying low as he approached the source of the smoke. It wasn't long before he saw it—a small, hastily constructed campsite hidden in a clearing.

A fire still smoldered in the center, the embers glowing faintly in the dim light. Around the fire, there were signs of recent activity: discarded food wrappers, empty water bottles, and the unmistakable glint of spent ammunition casings. Jack's jaw tightened. Whoever had been here was armed and dangerous, and they were close.

He scanned the perimeter, his eyes catching movement near the edge of the clearing. A figure emerged from the shadows, dressed in dark tactical gear, a rifle slung over his shoulder. The man moved with the precision of a trained soldier, his eyes scanning the area as if expecting trouble.

Jack's mind raced. He could take the man out—silent and quick—but there was no telling how many others were nearby. He had to be smart about this. He retreated slowly, careful not to make a sound as he melted back into the forest.

As he moved further away from the camp, Jack's heart pounded in his chest. This was worse than he had thought. The island wasn't just being used as a drop-off point; it was a base of operations. And if there were this many men here, it meant they were gearing up for something big.

Jack's mind went back to the women. They had said more men were coming—likely to collect the next shipment. If Jack was going to stop them, he had to act fast. But going in guns blazing wasn't an option, not without knowing exactly what he was up against.

He reached the edge of the forest and stopped, his hands resting on his knees as he took a moment to catch his breath. His heart was still racing, but his mind was sharp, focused. He needed a plan.

Jack looked back toward the cabin. The women were counting on him, whether he liked it or not. And as much as he wanted to run, to leave this whole mess behind, he knew he couldn't. Not this time.

He stood up straight, the weight of the decision settling on his shoulders. He would fight. But he'd fight on his terms. He'd use the island to his advantage, just like he had been taught in his SEAL training. It was time to stir the waters and flush these bastards out, one by one.

With a final glance at the forest, Jack turned and headed back toward the cabin. There was no turning back now.

Jack Kincaid wasn't one to ignore his instincts. Years of training and a life built on split-second decisions made sure of that. Standing by as a criminal syndicate used the island as a playground for smuggling wasn't an option. His isolation had been a refuge from the world and, more importantly, from himself, but the arrival of the trafficked women washed ashore changed everything. He could feel the old fire flickering deep within him, urging him to act.

As the sun began its descent beyond the horizon, Jack set out to investigate. The island, rugged and mostly untouched by human hands, stretched in all directions like a fortress built by nature itself. Dense forests lined the hills, and sharp cliffs jutted out over the ocean, creating the perfect hiding places for anyone looking to remain undetected.

He moved swiftly but cautiously through the forest. His boots left shallow prints in the dirt, the only sign he had even passed through. The island had become his domain over the last few years, and he knew every trail, every nook where the terrain gave way to potential hiding spots. Yet, the weight of knowing something darker was festering here made the air feel heavier. It wasn't just his sanctuary anymore.

The first sign of activity was subtle, almost imperceptible: footprints that weren't his own, leading deeper into the interior of the island. Jack crouched down, running his fingers through the disturbed earth. He wasn't looking at the footprint but at its depth, the spacing between steps, and the wear on the surrounding plants. A small group had passed through here recently, and they were carrying weight—likely supplies.

Standing up, he followed the tracks further inland, where the ground sloped upward. His senses remained on high alert, the quiet tension building inside him. Every rustle of the leaves could be a potential threat, every broken branch a sign that someone else was moving nearby. But for now, the forest seemed still.

After an hour of trekking, Jack came upon a small clearing. Hidden among the trees, there was an abandoned campsite. His eyes narrowed. The smuggling ring had been here. That much was clear. Empty food cans and discarded cigarette butts littered the ground. They hadn't left in a hurry, which meant they didn't expect anyone to find this spot.

He crouched down by a makeshift fire pit, rubbing the ashes between his fingers. The fire had been out for at least a day, maybe more, but the wind hadn't scattered the remnants yet. As his gaze traveled upward, Jack noticed a camouflaged tarp tied between two trees. It had been used to conceal something, but what?

His heart pounded as he lifted the tarp to find several crates hidden beneath. Breaking open the first one, Jack's suspicions were confirmed—these weren't supplies for surviving on the island. Inside, there were military-grade weapons, tightly packed and ready for transport. AK-47s, ammunition, and grenades. Not the kind of gear any local group would need. This was big. Much bigger than he had anticipated.

The crates bore no insignia or markings that could easily identify them, but Jack didn't need that to know where they had come from. He'd seen these kinds of shipments before, in places where governments had no jurisdiction and everything was for sale to the highest bidder.

As he surveyed the other crates, he noticed something that made his blood run cold—a hidden compartment in the largest box. Sliding it open, Jack's stomach twisted when he saw what was inside: binders filled with photographs, ledgers, and maps. Each one meticulously detailed the operations taking place on the island. The maps showed routes, locations where shipments were received, and drop-off points around the coast.

The photographs were the worst. Images of terrified faces—women, children, and men—shackled in makeshift holding areas, waiting to be sold. Some of the faces looked familiar, and his gut told him they were the same women who had washed ashore. This wasn't just a smuggling operation. It was human trafficking on an industrial scale. And the island was the staging ground for their latest enterprise.

Jack's fingers tightened around the binder. He had to get this evidence back to the women. They needed to see just how deep the operation went and understand the danger that still lingered. But as he closed the crate, his trained senses picked up something else—movement. The faint crack of a branch somewhere behind him, just beyond the treeline.

His hand went instinctively to the knife strapped to his waist. He wasn't alone. Staying low, Jack slipped silently into the underbrush, moving like a shadow toward the sound. His muscles tensed, each step careful and deliberate as he maneuvered through the dense vegetation. The faint light filtering through the canopy above didn't offer much in the way of clarity, but his hearing more than made up for it.

Another footfall. Closer this time.

Peering through a break in the foliage, Jack saw them—two men. Armed, alert, and wearing tactical gear. They moved with the precision of trained operatives, but their focus was split. They weren't looking for him; they were on patrol. The smuggling operation had sent men to check on the hidden cache. Jack's mind raced. If they discovered the empty camp and noticed the opened crate, they'd know someone was on the island. He couldn't let that happen.

With silent precision, Jack calculated the distance between them and him. He had a narrow window of opportunity. If he moved too soon, he'd alert the other, but if he waited, they'd be too close to the weapons stash. Timing was everything.

The first man approached within ten feet of Jack's position, oblivious to the fact he was being stalked. Jack moved quickly, stepping out from the brush like a predator striking from the shadows. He grabbed the man's head, covering his mouth and wrenching him backward in one swift motion. The knife did its work before the man could make a sound, and his body fell limp into the undergrowth.

The second mercenary barely had time to react before Jack was on him. The man's gun came up too late. Jack knocked it aside and delivered a crushing blow to his throat. He gagged, stumbling backward, but Jack didn't relent. Within moments, the second mercenary lay crumpled next to his comrade, unconscious.

Jack exhaled quietly, checking the surroundings again for any further threats. But the forest was silent once more, save for the rustle of wind through the leaves. He took a moment to go through their gear. Both men had radios, small arms, and combat knives. Professional, but not elite. These weren't military. They were hired guns, working for whoever paid the most.

But one thing stood out—an insignia on the inner pocket of one of the men's jackets. It was subtle, nearly invisible to anyone not looking for it, but Jack recognized it immediately. His pulse quickened.

The Colonel.

It was a name Jack hadn't uttered in years, a man he thought had died in the same hellhole mission that had destroyed his life. But seeing that insignia, the world shifted.

The Colonel was alive. And not only was he alive, but he was running this entire operation.

The betrayal Jack felt during that failed mission had haunted him ever since. His commander had left him and his team for dead, and now the man was orchestrating a human trafficking and smuggling operation. The Colonel had gone from a government asset to a criminal kingpin, and Jack was standing in the middle of his operation.

He clenched his fists, the weight of it all crashing down on him. His mission was clear now. He wasn't just dismantling a smuggling ring—he was going after the man who had ruined his life.

With no time to waste, Jack hoisted the two unconscious bodies into a thicket where they wouldn't be immediately visible. He took their radios and weapons, knowing they would prove useful later.

As night fell, Jack made his way back to the isolated cave where the trafficked women were hiding. He had avoided most of the island's more open spaces, sticking to the shadows and moving with the kind of stealth only a trained operator could achieve.

When he reached the women, he saw the fear etched on their faces. One of the women, Elena, the one who seemed to speak for the group, looked at him with a mixture of relief and terror.

"Did you find anything?" she asked, her voice trembling.

Jack nodded grimly and handed her the binder. As she opened it and began to sift through the pages, her face went pale. The other women crowded around, their eyes widening in horror at the photographs and the detailed notes that confirmed the extent of the operation.

"This... this is worse than we thought," Elena whispered, her voice cracking.

Jack sat down, wiping the sweat and grime from his brow. "It's bigger than just this island. The Colonel, the man behind this... he's not going to stop until someone forces him to."

"And what about us? What happens now?" another woman asked, her voice barely audible.

Jack looked at them, seeing the desperation in their eyes. He had been alone for so long, drifting through life without a purpose. But now, standing at the precipice of something far bigger than himself, he realized he couldn't turn back.

"You're not alone," Jack said firmly. "I'll get you off this island, but first... I need to finish what I started."

The room was silent, the weight of his words sinking in. Jack had no illusions about what lay ahead. The Colonel's reach extended far beyond this island, and Jack knew that by challenging him, he was declaring war. But for the first time in years, Jack felt a sense of purpose. The Colonel had stolen his past, but Jack wasn't going to let him steal anyone else's future.

With renewed resolve, Jack stood, his eyes scanning the darkening sky outside. The Colonel had to be stopped. And this time, Jack wasn't just fighting for himself.

He was fighting for them.

Chapter 3: Ghosts of the Past

The morning fog clung to the trees like a heavy veil, muting the already subdued colors of the island. Jack Kincaid moved silently through the dense undergrowth, his senses heightened as he followed a barely discernible trail deeper into the forest. The island, his solitary refuge for years, now felt unfamiliar, as if it had taken on a new, darker life in the wake of the storm. His mind kept drifting back to the trafficked women, their haunted faces etched with fear and desperation. But what troubled him more was their story—about the smuggling operation that used this island as a hidden base.

Jack had spent the last few days scouting, relying on his training to search for clues, and what he'd found disturbed him. Abandoned campsites, hidden supply caches, and recent tracks indicated that someone had been moving through the island unnoticed. His island. It made his skin crawl to think that they could've been operating under his nose for God knows how long. But this wasn't just any smuggling ring. There was something personal about it, something that made his gut churn in ways he hadn't felt since the Navy.

The weight of his rifle was a familiar comfort slung across his back as he crouched low near a ridge, scanning the landscape below. The thick foliage thinned out, revealing a small, makeshift airstrip—the kind used for quick in-and-out operations. His heart quickened. Jack knew this wasn't some random setup; it was organized, meticulous. Whoever was behind this had military precision. He felt the old instincts rising, pushing through the haze of his self-imposed exile. This was no longer about whether or not he should get involved. He was involved now, like it or not.

As he moved closer to the airstrip, Jack's eyes caught movement. He froze, blending into the landscape like a shadow, his breath shallow and controlled. A group of men, heavily armed, appeared from the treeline, their gear too high-end for local thugs. These were professionals. Jack's mind raced, processing every detail—their formation, their weaponry, their relaxed yet purposeful demeanor. They weren't expecting trouble. That made sense. This was their territory, after all.

But then, his eyes locked onto a figure toward the back of the group, a man who moved with a slight limp, his face partially obscured by a baseball cap pulled low. There was something disturbingly familiar about him. Jack's pulse quickened, and he felt the muscles in his jaw tighten. He shifted slightly to get a better view, careful not to make a sound.

The man stopped, barking orders at the others, his voice rough and commanding. And then it hit Jack like a punch to the gut. He knew that voice. He knew that limp.

For a moment, time seemed to stop. His mind struggled to reconcile what he was seeing with what he knew to be true. The man was supposed to be dead. Jack had watched him die, or so he thought. Years ago, during that disastrous mission—the mission—Jack had seen the bodies, had felt the crushing weight of responsibility for their deaths. But there he was, alive.

The man was Frank Barlow, a ghost from Jack's past. Barlow had been part of the same SEAL team on that fateful mission, a man Jack had trusted with his life. But Barlow hadn't made it out, or at least, that's what Jack had believed for years. He remembered the explosion, the chaos, and the bodies being dragged away in the aftermath. The mission had gone sideways, civilians had been killed, and their team had been disbanded in the wake of the scandal. Jack had blamed himself, had been haunted by the faces of the dead—especially the child.

And now, Barlow was here, alive and very much involved in this smuggling operation. Jack's mind raced as he pieced together the implications. Barlow's presence wasn't a coincidence. He hadn't just survived; he had switched sides. He was working for them, whoever they were.

Jack's hand instinctively moved to the grip of his rifle, his knuckles whitening with the tension. His heart pounded in his chest, the flood of emotions—betrayal, anger, confusion—threatening to overwhelm him. But he forced himself to breathe, to think. This wasn't the time for rash decisions. Not yet.

He watched as the group began loading crates onto an old cargo plane, clearly preparing for some kind of transfer. Jack stayed still, studying the operation with the precision of a hunter. There were at least six men, all armed. Too many for him to take out alone, not without backup. But Jack didn't have backup, not anymore. This wasn't the SEALs, and there wasn't a team waiting to extract him if things went south.

His mind drifted to the trafficked women. They had been terrified when they arrived, and now Jack understood why. This was no small-time operation. It was part of something much larger, and if Barlow was involved, that meant only one thing: The Colonel.

The name was like a slap in the face, dragging him back to memories he had tried to bury. The Colonel had been their commanding officer, the one who had sent them on that mission—who had betrayed them when everything went wrong. Jack had thought he was dead too, or at least out of the picture. But if Barlow was here, it meant The Colonel couldn't be far behind. He was the puppet master, pulling the strings from behind the scenes.

Jack's hands clenched into fists. His exile, his isolation, had been a way to escape the ghosts of his past, to punish himself for the lives lost, for his failure. But now those ghosts were right here, staring him in the face. He wasn't ready for this. He wasn't ready to confront the man who had destroyed his career, his life. But what choice did he have?

The decision made itself. Jack couldn't walk away, not now. He couldn't let these men continue their operation, trafficking drugs, weapons, and innocent lives. And he couldn't let The Colonel get away with it.

He would have to act, but he needed more information first. Jack slipped back into the cover of the trees, moving as silently as he had when he was still part of the SEALs. He knew the island better than they did, and that gave him the advantage. For now.

He would watch, wait, and learn. And when the time was right, he would strike.

Hours passed as Jack tracked the mercenaries from a distance. They moved like a well-oiled machine, unloading the crates with precision and setting up a temporary camp near the airstrip. Jack kept his distance, observing every detail. He noted their weapons, their routines, the way they communicated. He also made note of the cargo—wooden crates marked with symbols he didn't recognize. He couldn't be sure if they were filled with drugs, weapons, or something worse. But it didn't matter. Whatever was inside, it wasn't good.

As the sun dipped lower in the sky, casting long shadows across the island, Jack knew he had to make a decision. He couldn't take on all of them at once, but if he could isolate one of them—preferably Barlow—he might be able to get some answers. The Colonel was the real target, but Barlow would know how to get to him.

The thought of confronting Barlow made Jack's blood boil. The man had been a brother to him, someone he had trusted with his life. And now he was working for the enemy. Jack wanted to put a bullet in him, but he knew that wouldn't get him the information he needed. Not yet, anyway.

As the mercenaries settled into their camp for the night, Jack saw his opportunity. Barlow had wandered off from the group, his limp more pronounced as he moved toward the edge of the camp, probably to relieve himself. Jack's pulse quickened. This was his chance.

Moving like a shadow, Jack crept through the undergrowth, using the noise of the wind and the distant crash of waves to mask his approach. Barlow was alone, his back to Jack, completely unaware of the danger closing in.

In one swift motion, Jack was on him, a hand clamped over Barlow's mouth as he dragged him into the trees. Barlow struggled, but Jack was stronger, pinning him against a tree with brutal efficiency.

"Shut up," Jack growled, his voice low and dangerous. "If you make a sound, I'll snap your neck."

Barlow's eyes widened in recognition as he stared at Jack. For a moment, there was only shock, then something else—fear. He tried to speak, but Jack's hand was still over his mouth.

"You're going to answer my questions, Barlow," Jack whispered, his face inches from the man's. "And if you lie to me, I'll know."

Jack slowly removed his hand, but kept his grip on Barlow, ready to strike if he tried anything.

"You're supposed to be dead," Barlow rasped, his voice shaky.

"Funny," Jack said, his voice cold. "I was about to say the same thing about you."

Jack Kincaid's heart pounded in his chest as he crouched behind the jagged rocks, the dense foliage of the island's jungle providing scant cover. He had always prided himself on being able to stay one step ahead of danger, but this was different. The revelation of his former commanding officer's involvement in the smuggling operation was a blow that shook him to his core. The weight of it pressed heavily on his shoulders, making each breath feel labored and each movement fraught with tension.

The Colonel—Jack's old boss, the man who had been a mentor, a leader, and then, the very embodiment of betrayal. The news that he was the head of this illicit network of human traffickers, arms dealers, and drug smugglers was an ugly twist of fate. Jack could hardly believe it. The man he had once respected, who had turned his back on him during that fateful mission, was now the architect of so much suffering.

Jack's mind raced as he processed this grim reality. The Colonel's name was synonymous with duty and honor in Jack's memory, but now it was tied to corruption, cruelty, and a betrayal that cut deeper than he'd ever imagined. He needed to understand how The Colonel had risen to such power and, more importantly, how to bring him down.

He had been following the mercenaries for days, carefully observing their routines, their patrols, and their operations. Their camp was a hive of activity, with armed guards stationed at key points, and a heavily fortified perimeter. The mercenaries were well-organized, their movements precise and their demeanor intimidating. Jack had avoided direct contact, relying on his training to remain hidden. But now, knowing that The Colonel was at the center of this operation, he couldn't stay on the sidelines any longer.

Jack's plan was simple: gather as much information as possible about The Colonel's operations and identify his weaknesses. If he was going to take down this smuggling ring, he needed to understand the structure, the supply chains, and, most importantly, The Colonel's whereabouts and plans.

The sun had dipped below the horizon, and the jungle was enveloped in a thick darkness. Jack moved silently through the underbrush, his senses sharp, every rustle of leaves and snap of twigs registering in his mind. He reached a vantage point overlooking the central area of the camp. Through the gaps in the foliage, he could see several structures, including a large, reinforced building that was likely The Colonel's headquarters.

The camp was illuminated by sparse, flickering lights, casting long shadows that danced ominously. Jack's binoculars revealed a mix of faces: hardened mercenaries, some wearing tactical gear, others in more casual attire but still armed. They moved with the practiced ease of men who knew their territory and their enemies. Jack recognized a few of them from his military past, although they had been mere shadows during his time in the field.

His gaze was drawn back to the central building. There was something distinctly different about it—an aura of authority and control. If The Colonel was indeed inside, this was where Jack would find him. But the building was surrounded by guards and was more heavily fortified than the other structures in the camp.

Jack needed a strategy, and he needed it fast. His first priority was to get inside the building without alerting the guards. He had seen a small maintenance tunnel on the side of the structure during his earlier reconnaissance. It was likely used for ventilation or waste disposal and could serve as an entry point.

He waited for the right moment—when the guards' attention was diverted and the camp's activity reached its peak. It was a risky move, but one that Jack was willing to make. He took advantage of the chaos caused by a loud argument among the mercenaries, slipping through the shadows toward the tunnel entrance.

The tunnel was narrow and dark, filled with the stench of mildew and decay. Jack moved swiftly but cautiously, making his way through the dimly lit passage. The tunnel led him to a utility room within the building. Jack emerged quietly, taking stock of his surroundings. He could hear muffled voices from the next room—an indication that he was getting closer to his target.

He crept forward, careful to avoid making any noise. The room was sparsely furnished, with only a few crates and barrels stacked against the walls. Jack approached a door that led to the next area, pressing his ear against it to listen. The voices were clearer now, and he could make out two distinct tones. One was authoritative, commanding, and the other was more subdued, almost pleading.

Jack's heart skipped a beat. Could it be The Colonel in the other room? There was only one way to find out. He took a deep breath, prepared for whatever lay beyond the door, and slowly turned the handle. The door creaked open, revealing a dimly lit office.

The room was filled with maps, documents, and surveillance equipment. It was clear that this was a command center of sorts. And there, behind a large desk covered in papers, sat The Colonel. His back was to Jack, but there was no mistaking the silhouette or the authoritative posture. Jack's breath caught in his throat.

The Colonel was speaking with someone on a secure phone, his voice low and steady. Jack moved closer, inching along the wall until he was close enough to hear the conversation.

"... and make sure the shipment leaves tonight," The Colonel said. "We can't afford any delays. The authorities are getting too close."

The voice on the other end responded, but the words were indistinguishable. The Colonel's words were laced with a mix of urgency and menace, a stark contrast to the man Jack had once known. He seemed more like a shadowy figure than the leader he had once admired.

As The Colonel hung up the phone, Jack's heart pounded louder. He had to make his move before it was too late. The Colonel was about to leave the room, and Jack knew he had only a few seconds to act. He surveyed the room for anything that could aid him in his mission. There was a file cabinet in the corner, its drawers stuffed with documents. Jack needed to gather as much intel as possible before he confronted The Colonel.

With practiced speed, Jack rifled through the cabinet, pulling out files and photographs. Most of them were related to the smuggling operation—lists of contacts, shipment schedules, and maps of the island. Jack's fingers skimmed over a particularly detailed map of the island, noting the locations of hidden caches and supply routes.

He heard footsteps approaching and knew he had to act quickly. Jack stuffed the documents into his bag and prepared to leave. As he turned to exit, he heard the door to the office swing open. Without thinking, Jack ducked behind the desk, his heart racing.

The Colonel entered the room, accompanied by a burly man Jack didn't recognize. Their conversation was heated, filled with terms and names that Jack couldn't immediately place. But the tension was palpable. The Colonel's demeanor was colder and more calculating than Jack remembered.

"I don't want any more surprises," The Colonel said, his voice edged with anger. "If this shipment is delayed, we'll have serious problems."

The other man nodded, his face tense. "We're moving as fast as we can. The authorities are already getting suspicious."

Jack listened intently, piecing together the fragments of their conversation. The Colonel was clearly anxious about the impending shipment and the scrutiny it was attracting. This was an opportunity Jack couldn't afford to miss.

As the two men continued to talk, Jack made his move. He slipped out from behind the desk and quietly headed towards the exit. His heart was still pounding, but he felt a surge of determination. He had gathered crucial information—information that would be invaluable in dismantling The Colonel's operation.

Jack made his way back through the utility tunnel, retracing his steps with the same caution he had used to enter. The documents in his bag were a potential goldmine, and he knew he needed to get them to the women who had washed ashore. They could help him understand the full scope of the operation and offer insights into the smuggling network.

Once outside, Jack disappeared into the dense jungle, his mind racing with thoughts of what lay ahead. The Colonel's involvement in the operation was a game-changer. It meant that Jack wasn't just up against a criminal network but against a man who had once been a mentor and had now become a symbol of betrayal and corruption.

Jack knew that taking down The Colonel would be no easy task. The man had built an empire of deceit and had surrounded himself with loyal, dangerous mercenaries. But

Jack had something the Colonel didn't—an unwavering sense of justice and a determination to see this mission through to the end.

As he made his way back to his makeshift camp, Jack resolved to use the information he had gathered to plan his next move. The fight against The Colonel was just beginning, and Jack was prepared to do whatever it took to see it through. The ghosts of his past were no longer just haunting memories—they were now the driving force behind his quest for redemption.

Jack Kincaid had always been a man of action, and this was no different. With each step he took, he felt the weight of his past and the responsibility of his present merging into a single, unstoppable force. The Colonel had made a grave mistake by involving Jack in this operation, and Jack was determined to make him pay.

The island, once a sanctuary of solitude, had become the battleground for Jack's fight against corruption and betrayal. As the night enveloped the island in darkness, Jack prepared for the challenges that lay ahead, knowing that the true confrontation with The Colonel was yet to come.

Chapter 4: Lines Drawn

The island had become a dark and treacherous world, a labyrinth of shadows and hidden dangers. For Jack Kincaid, it was no longer just a place of solitude and penance—it was a battleground, a place where he had to confront the ghosts of his past and the formidable criminal network led by The Colonel.

Jack's latest reconnaissance had made it painfully clear: The Colonel's smuggling operation was more expansive and sinister than he had initially imagined. What he had once thought of as a rogue operation was, in fact, a well-oiled machine of criminality, operating with ruthless efficiency and deep-seated corruption.

The Colonel had established a network that spanned the island, with multiple layers of security, hidden caches of weapons and drugs, and a constant flow of human trafficking. Jack could see the signs of it everywhere—abandoned camps, fortified compounds, and secretive meetings. The scale of the operation was staggering, and the more Jack uncovered, the more he realized that taking down this network would be a monumental task.

The map he had obtained from The Colonel's office revealed a series of interconnected locations across the island. There were primary and secondary camps, hidden bunkers, and a central hub—the main base where The Colonel resided. Each location was meticulously mapped out, with routes and supply lines clearly marked. This was a treasure trove of information, but it also made Jack's mission clear: he needed to disrupt this operation systematically, one piece at a time.

Jack had spent the last few days planning his next move. His strategy was to create chaos within the operation, to hit the network at its weakest points, and to force The Colonel into the open. He knew he couldn't take down the entire operation at once—he had to be methodical, careful, and above all, patient.

He had identified three key targets: the supply depot, the trafficking center, and the communication hub. Each of these sites was critical to the operation's success and would yield significant results if disrupted. By taking them out, Jack hoped to create a ripple effect that would destabilize the entire network.

The first target was the supply depot. It was located in a heavily forested area, a few miles from the central camp. Jack had observed it from a distance, noting its defenses and the routines of the guards. It was a crucial site where weapons and drugs were stored before being distributed. Destroying it would severely impact the operation's ability to maintain its supply chain.

Jack prepared for the mission meticulously. He packed a bag with essential equipment: a silenced pistol, a high-powered rifle, explosives, and a set of lock-picking tools. He also carried a few survival essentials—water, rations, and a first-aid kit. His goal was to be in and out quickly, leaving no trace of his presence.

The journey to the depot was fraught with danger. Jack moved silently through the dense jungle, his senses on high alert. Every rustle of leaves, every snap of a twig, was a potential threat. He had to navigate carefully, avoiding patrols and surveillance. The terrain was rugged, with uneven ground and thick undergrowth that made movement slow and difficult.

As he approached the supply depot, Jack used his night vision goggles to survey the area. The depot was surrounded by a high fence topped with razor wire. Guard towers with spotlights provided a clear view of the perimeter, and armed guards patrolled the area in a regular pattern. Jack noted the guard schedules, timing his movements to coincide with the moments when the guards were furthest from their posts.

The depot itself was a large, metal warehouse with several smaller storage buildings scattered around it. Jack's plan was to plant explosives on the main warehouse, causing a large enough explosion to attract attention and create confusion. The secondary buildings, where the weapons and drugs were stored, would be left intact but heavily damaged.

He approached the fence, using his wire cutters to create a small opening. He crawled through, staying low to avoid detection. Once inside the perimeter, he made his way to the warehouse, using the cover of darkness to remain hidden. He carefully planted the explosives in strategic locations, ensuring that the blast would be both powerful and controlled.

The most challenging part of the mission was yet to come: getting out without being detected. Jack knew that the explosion would draw attention, and he had to be far from the site before it happened. He retraced his steps, moving quickly through the jungle. As he reached a safe distance, he set the timer on the explosives and took cover.

The explosion rocked the night, sending a plume of smoke and debris into the air. Jack could hear the shouts and cries of the guards as they scrambled to respond. The sound of sirens and gunfire filled the air, signaling that his plan had worked. The depot was in chaos, and Jack had successfully caused a significant disruption.

With the first target complete, Jack turned his attention to the trafficking center. This site was more difficult to access, located near the coast and heavily guarded. The trafficking center was where the human lives were traded like commodities, and Jack had vowed to do everything in his power to stop it.

He had obtained information from the women who had washed ashore, who had described the trafficking center in detail. It was a grim place, with makeshift cells and a constant stream of victims being brought in and out. Jack's plan was to liberate as many captives as possible and dismantle the center's operations.

The trafficking center was located in a remote area, accessible only by a narrow, winding road. Jack had to approach it carefully, avoiding detection and scouting the perimeter. The center was guarded by a mix of mercenaries and local thugs, all armed and on high alert.

Jack waited for nightfall before making his move. Using the cover of darkness, he approached the center's perimeter, cutting through the fence with precision. He moved silently, disabling the security cameras and avoiding the guards. His goal was to get inside, find the captives, and free them without alerting the entire facility.

Inside the center, Jack found a grim scene. The captives were housed in small, filthy cells, their faces etched with fear and despair. Jack worked quickly, unlocking the cells and leading the captives to safety. He had prepared a safe house for them, a place where they could find refuge until he could arrange for their rescue.

The operation at the trafficking center was risky and fraught with danger, but Jack was determined to make a difference. He managed to free several captives, providing them with basic necessities and ensuring their safety. He also gathered valuable intelligence on the center's operations, including the routes used to transport victims and the identities of key players in the trafficking ring.

With the trafficking center compromised, Jack turned his attention to the communication hub. This was the nerve center of the operation, where all the information and coordination took place. It was a heavily fortified building, located near the central camp.

The communication hub was crucial to The Colonel's operation, as it allowed him to coordinate movements, manage logistics, and maintain control over his network. Jack's plan was to disable the hub, cutting off The Colonel's ability to communicate and coordinate his forces.

He approached the hub cautiously, using his knowledge of the island's layout to avoid detection. The building was equipped with state-of-the-art security systems, including biometric scanners and encrypted communications. Jack had to use all his skills to bypass these defenses and gain access to the hub.

Inside, Jack found a complex array of computer systems and communication equipment. He worked quickly, planting explosives and disabling the equipment. The goal was to cause a major disruption, preventing The Colonel from coordinating his operations and forcing him to react to the chaos.

As he set the final charges, Jack heard the sound of footsteps approaching. He knew he had to leave quickly. He made his way out of the building, retracing his steps and avoiding the guards. The explosion would create a significant disturbance, and Jack had to be far from the site before it happened.

The communication hub was soon engulfed in flames, with a thick plume of smoke rising into the night sky. Jack could hear the sounds of confusion and alarm as The Colonel's network scrambled to respond. The disruption was significant, and Jack had achieved another key objective.

With the communication hub disabled and the trafficking center compromised, Jack had made a major impact on The Colonel's operation. But the battle was far from over. He knew that The Colonel would retaliate and that the fight was only beginning.

Jack returned to his temporary camp, exhausted but determined. He had disrupted the operation, but he still had a long way to go. The Colonel's network was vast, and there were many more targets to hit. Jack needed to stay focused and continue his efforts to dismantle the smuggling ring and bring The Colonel to justice.

As Jack sat by the fire, he reviewed the intelligence he had gathered. The Colonel's operation was complex and deeply entrenched, but Jack was committed to seeing it through. He knew that the stakes were high and that every action he took would have a significant impact on the outcome of his mission.

The island was now a battleground, and Jack was in the thick of it. He had made significant progress, but the fight was far from over. The Colonel was still out there, and Jack knew that the final confrontation would be the ultimate test of his skills and determination.

As the night wore on, Jack prepared for the challenges that lay ahead. He had disrupted The Colonel's operation, but he knew that the real battle was yet to come. The fight for justice and redemption was far from over, and Jack was ready to face whatever came next.

The tropical night was still, save for the distant hum of insects and the occasional rustle of the wind through the dense foliage. The moon cast a silver veil over the deserted island, turning the ocean into a glimmering, dark expanse. Jack Kincaid crouched on the edge of a cliff overlooking the coastline, his eyes scanning the darkness. He had spent the last few hours in this position, gathering what little intelligence he could on the smuggling operation and the men who were part of it.

The revelation that his former commanding officer, The Colonel, was behind the operation was like a blade slicing through the fog of his past. The sheer weight of betrayal, combined with the realization that the network was dealing in drugs, weapons, and human lives, was almost unbearable. Jack had always thought that the worst of his failures was behind him, but now, he faced a new set of demons.

He reached into his tactical vest and pulled out a worn map of the island. By moonlight, he traced the routes he had uncovered so far—trails leading to hidden camps, abandoned warehouses, and signs of recent activity. The island was more than just a remote outpost; it was a well-hidden base of operations. The dense jungle provided perfect cover for illicit activities, and the cliffs and rocky coastline made it difficult for any unwanted guests to approach unnoticed.

Jack's thoughts were interrupted by the soft crunch of footsteps behind him. He turned, his hand instinctively going to the knife strapped to his side. In the dim light, he saw Anna, one of the survivors who had washed ashore. Her eyes were wide with fear and determination. She had been one of the most vocal in pleading for Jack's help, and her presence now was a reminder of the stakes involved.

"Jack, are you sure you want to do this?" she asked, her voice barely above a whisper. "This isn't just about saving us anymore. You're taking on an entire network. They'll kill you if they find out."

Jack's eyes hardened. "If I don't act, they'll keep doing what they've been doing. It's not just about saving you and the others. It's about stopping a whole operation that's destroying lives."

Anna nodded, her expression one of grim acceptance. She had seen enough to understand that Jack's decision was final. "What's the plan?"

Jack unfolded the map, pointing to several locations. "There are three main areas of interest: the warehouse near the north shore, the underground bunker in the southern jungle, and the communication hub near the cliffs. Each one plays a different role in their operation. I need to hit them one by one, disrupt their logistics, and gather whatever intel I can."

Anna studied the map, her face pale but resolute. "I can help with the survivors. There are still others who need medical attention. If you're going to go after them, we need to make sure we're safe here. I know a bit about medicine. Maybe I can find some supplies and make sure they're secure."

Jack considered her offer. While he hadn't initially planned on involving her in his mission, her determination and willingness to help could be an asset. "Alright. You stay here and keep the survivors safe. I'll start with the warehouse tonight. If I'm not back by dawn, assume the worst and get them off the island."

Anna nodded, her face set in determination. "Be careful, Jack. They're not just criminals. They're organized, and they're ruthless."

Jack gave her a curt nod and set off, moving silently through the underbrush. The island's night was alive with sounds—the screeches of nocturnal creatures, the distant crash of waves against the cliffs, and the whisper of the wind. Jack's mind was focused, his every sense tuned to the task ahead.

The warehouse was located on the northern edge of the island, nestled among a cluster of trees. Jack approached it cautiously, his movements practiced and deliberate. The facility was a large, nondescript structure with no visible windows and a single, heavy door. The smuggling operation's presence here was evident in the large crates stacked outside, marked with symbols Jack recognized from the intelligence he'd gathered.

He moved around the perimeter, looking for an entry point. The door was guarded, with two men patrolling the area. Jack surveyed their movements, noting their routines and weaknesses. The guards were armed and seemed alert, but Jack's training had taught him to exploit even the smallest of lapses.

He decided to take them out quietly. With the stealth of a predator, Jack approached the first guard, who was leaning against a crate, distracted by a cigarette. Jack's silent approach was barely a whisper in the night. He slipped behind the man and, with a swift, practiced motion, incapacitated him without a sound. The guard fell silently to the ground, and Jack quickly disposed of his body, hiding it behind a stack of crates.

The second guard was more alert, pacing back and forth with a sense of purpose. Jack waited until the guard was facing away, then moved in. He had to be quicker this time, his movements a blur of efficiency. With a chokehold that left no room for resistance, Jack subdued the second guard and hid him alongside his partner.

With the path clear, Jack moved to the warehouse door. It was locked, but Jack had anticipated this. He pulled out his lock-picking tools and, within minutes, had the door open. The interior was dimly lit, with the faint hum of generators providing the only illumination. Jack's eyes quickly adjusted to the darkness, and he began his search.

The warehouse was filled with crates and barrels, some marked with the same symbols he had seen outside, others with labels indicating pharmaceuticals and chemicals. Jack knew he needed to be thorough. He moved methodically through the rows, opening crates and inspecting their contents. His efforts were rewarded when he found a stash of documents and a laptop tucked away in a corner.

Jack quickly set up a small workstation, connecting the laptop to his own encrypted device. As he sifted through the files, he found detailed logs of shipments, communication records, and a list of personnel involved in the operation. The documents were a goldmine of information, but time was running short. He knew he couldn't stay long.

As he was about to finish, a sudden noise made him freeze. Footsteps were approaching. Jack's heart raced as he quickly shut down the laptop and stashed the documents in his bag. He crept toward the entrance, peering through a small window. A group of men, armed and talking animatedly, were heading toward the warehouse. Jack recognized some of them as mercenaries he had seen before.

He had to act fast. Jack retreated deeper into the warehouse, finding a vantage point behind a stack of crates. The men entered, their voices growing louder as they discussed their plans. Jack could hear snippets of conversation about an upcoming shipment and the need for increased security.

He waited, every muscle in his body tense as the men moved about the warehouse, checking inventory and discussing their operations. Jack used the opportunity to gather as much information as he could, his mind working furiously to piece together the puzzle. The more he learned, the clearer the scope of the smuggling ring became. They were not just dealing in drugs and weapons; their operation was far-reaching, with connections to powerful figures and dangerous organizations.

When the men finally left, Jack exhaled slowly, his body relaxing from the tense crouch. He knew he had to leave quickly. With the documents and laptop secured, he retraced his steps, avoiding any further encounters. The night air was cool against his face as he emerged from the warehouse and made his way back through the jungle.

As Jack approached the makeshift camp where Anna and the other survivors were staying, he couldn't shake the feeling of being watched. The smuggling ring was extensive, and the more he uncovered, the more dangerous it became. But he was committed now. He had seen the suffering, and he had vowed to end it.

Anna was waiting for him, her face etched with concern. "What did you find?"

Jack handed her the documents and the laptop. "These contain everything we need to understand their operation. There's a lot more to this than just smuggling. They have connections that go all the way to the top."

Anna took the items, her eyes widening as she glanced through them. "This... this could bring them down."

Jack nodded. "That's the plan. But we're not out of danger yet. I need to hit the other locations. The bunker and the communication hub are next. If we can disrupt their operations there, it might be enough to make them slip up."

Anna's expression hardened with resolve. "I'll get to work on securing the survivors and organizing the supplies. But Jack, be careful. They know you're out there now. They'll be looking for you."

Jack nodded, his mind already moving to the next phase of his plan. He knew the risks were high, but there was no turning back now. With the documents and intel, he had a clearer picture of the operation, but the real challenge lay ahead. He had to dismantle the smuggling ring piece by piece, exposing the corruption and ensuring that justice was served.

As he set off into the night, Jack's thoughts were focused on the mission ahead. The Colonel's network was vast and dangerous, but Jack was determined. He had faced his past and was ready to confront the present. The stakes were higher than ever, but Jack knew that failure was not an option. The lives of the survivors and countless others depended on him. And Jack Kincaid was not one to back down from a fight.

Chapter 5: The Hunt Begins

Jack Kincaid moved silently through the dense undergrowth, his senses on high alert. The humid air was thick with the scent of decay, mingled with the faint aroma of salt from the surrounding ocean. The island, once a place of solitude and refuge, had become a battlefield, with Jack as its unlikely warrior. His days of isolation were over; now, he was immersed in a deadly game of cat and mouse.

The smuggling operation Jack was up against was not just a petty crime ring. It was a well-organized network with resources and manpower far beyond what he had initially anticipated. He had spent the past few days meticulously observing the activities of the mercenaries and scouring the island for any clues that might lead him to the heart of their operation.

Today, Jack's objective was to disrupt the smuggling ring's operations and create chaos within their ranks. He had already scouted several key locations: a hidden weapons cache, an abandoned communications post, and the areas where the mercenaries stored their supplies. Each discovery had given him more insight into the scale of the operation and the intricacies of its network.

Jack's training had taught him the importance of patience and precision. He had learned to be as much a shadow as a physical presence. Now, he applied those lessons with meticulous care. His plan was to use guerrilla tactics to sabotage the smuggling operation, striking at the heart of their logistics and communication.

His first target was a supply depot located deep in the forest. It was a small, nondescript building that had been hastily constructed and camouflaged. From his vantage point high in the trees, Jack could see the depot clearly. Two guards were stationed at the entrance, their weapons slung over their shoulders as they lazily chatted. Jack knew that taking out the guards would be the first step.

He reached into his pack and pulled out a silenced pistol, a tool he had managed to salvage from an abandoned weapons cache. With a slow, controlled breath, he lined up the sights and fired. The first guard dropped silently, a look of surprise frozen on his face. The second guard's reaction was more frantic, but Jack's second shot ensured he would not raise an alarm.

With the immediate threat neutralized, Jack moved swiftly to the depot's entrance. He used a small, specialized tool to pick the lock and slipped inside. The depot was cluttered with crates and barrels, most of them labeled with various markings that Jack knew were associated with illegal arms and drugs. His focus was on finding anything that might indicate where the Colonel was operating from or where the next shipment was heading.

He set up a small, portable camera to record the contents of the depot, intending to review it later for intelligence. For now, he focused on disabling the equipment. The smuggling ring relied heavily on communication and transportation, and disrupting these elements could cripple their operations.

Jack located the main power source for the depot's equipment and proceeded to sabotage it. He used a combination of explosive charges and careful dismantling to ensure that the equipment would be rendered useless. As he worked, he kept his ears open for any signs of reinforcements. The forest was quiet, but he knew better than to let his guard down.

Having completed the sabotage, Jack left the depot as silently as he had entered. His next move was to gather intelligence on the smuggling ring's network. He made his way to a location he had identified as a potential communications hub. This was another critical point in the operation, where the ring coordinated its activities and relayed information between its various cells.

The communications hub was set up in an old, abandoned building near the coast. Jack approached the structure with caution, using the cover of darkness to conceal his movements. He had studied the building's layout and knew the best entry points and potential hazards.

Inside, the hub was a hive of activity. The walls were lined with outdated but functional communication equipment, and several mercenaries were busy monitoring various screens and radios. Jack had to be careful; a direct confrontation here could be disastrous. Instead, he opted for a more subtle approach.

He used a small, remote-controlled drone to scout the interior of the building. The drone, equipped with a camera and a few basic tools, provided Jack with a real-time view of the operations. He noticed a series of encrypted messages being sent between different locations. This was the type of information that could be invaluable in disrupting the entire operation.

Jack hacked into the communications network using a portable device he had brought along. He was able to intercept and decode some of the messages, revealing the smuggling ring's upcoming plans. They were preparing for a large shipment that was due to arrive in a few days, a shipment that included both weapons and a new group of trafficked women.

With this information in hand, Jack decided to set up a series of traps to further disrupt the operation. His goal was to create a sense of paranoia and disorder within the smuggling ring, making it harder for them to coordinate their activities.

He rigged several key locations with makeshift explosives, carefully placing them in areas where they would cause the most disruption without endangering any civilians. The traps were set to trigger at various times, ensuring that the mercenaries would be kept on edge.

Jack's final task for the day was to retrieve the captured women he had encountered previously. They were being held in a makeshift camp hidden in a remote part of the island. He knew their situation was dire, and he wanted to make sure they were safe. The smuggling ring's operation relied heavily on fear and control, and freeing the captives would be a significant blow to their morale.

He approached the camp with the same stealth he had used for his previous operations. The camp was guarded, but Jack had carefully mapped out the guards' patrol routes and identified weak points in their defenses. Using the cover of darkness and his knowledge of their routines, he managed to neutralize the guards and liberate the women.

The women were scared and disoriented, but Jack's reassuring presence helped calm them. He led them to a safer location where he could ensure their safety until he could figure out a more permanent solution. As he sat with them, listening to their stories and learning more about the smuggling ring's activities, Jack realized the full extent of the operation's reach. The Colonel was not just running a local crime ring; he was part of a larger, more insidious network.

The night was long and tense. Jack knew that the smuggling ring would soon realize the extent of the damage he had inflicted. The traps, sabotage, and the freed captives were bound to provoke a reaction. He prepared himself for what was to come, knowing that the real battle was just beginning.

In the days that followed, Jack continued his campaign of disruption. He used every tool and tactic at his disposal to undermine the smuggling operation. His efforts were met with a mix of confusion, frustration, and increased aggression from the mercenaries. They were on high alert, and Jack could sense their growing desperation.

The stakes were high, and the pressure was mounting. Jack knew that he was pushing the smuggling ring to its limits. But he also knew that the Colonel was a cunning adversary, capable of adapting to any challenge. The real test would be in the final showdown, where Jack would have to confront the full force of the operation's defenses and bring the Colonel's empire crashing down.

For now, Jack was in his element. The isolation of the island had become a battleground where his skills and instincts were put to the ultimate test. The shadows of the forest were his allies, and every step he took was calculated to bring him closer to his ultimate goal. The hunt had begun, and Jack Kincaid was determined to see it through to the end.

Jack Kincaid stood in the dense foliage of the island's interior, sweat trickling down his back despite the cool evening breeze. The quiet of the forest was deceptive; beneath the surface, tension crackled like electricity. His thoughts churned, strategizing his next move against The Colonel's smuggling operation. His hands were steady, though his mind raced through the myriad of variables involved in the trap he was about to set.

For days, Jack had been dismantling the operation with guerrilla tactics—sabotaging equipment, eliminating key players, and keeping his presence a shadow. His actions had been swift and brutal, designed to inflict maximum damage while remaining undetected. But now, with The Colonel's network aware of an increasing threat, Jack needed to shift gears. He had to orchestrate a trap that would not only disrupt the operation but also force The Colonel's hand. His goal was to create a situation where The Colonel's men, driven by greed and desperation, would stumble into a carefully laid snare.

Jack had identified a crucial target: a shipment of supplies meant for an upcoming transaction. He knew this shipment was integral to The Colonel's operations, and capturing it would force the smugglers to react. The problem was how to lure them into a trap without alerting them too early. His plan involved setting up a decoy that would draw them in while ensuring he had the element of surprise.

The setting for his trap was a disused airstrip on the island's southern coast. The airstrip, abandoned for years, provided a perfect location for a covert exchange. The concrete was cracked, the hangar rusting, and the area secluded—ideal for Jack's purpose. He had been scouting it for days, noting the movements of The Colonel's men and planning his approach.

Jack's first task was to prepare the decoy. Using salvaged supplies, he rigged a small cache of valuable-looking equipment. To any observer, it would appear as if a major transaction was taking place. He placed several crates, stacked and wrapped with tarps, and wired them with rudimentary alarms that would trigger a small explosion if tampered with. The idea was to make it appear as though the cache was loaded with high-value contraband. He also set up motion sensors around the area, creating a perimeter that would alert him to any approach.

Satisfied with the setup, Jack retreated to a vantage point overlooking the airstrip. From there, he could see everything that transpired while remaining hidden. He had chosen a secluded spot in the trees, camouflaged by undergrowth, with a clear view of the strip and the surrounding area.

As the sun dipped below the horizon, the forest darkened, and the air grew cooler. Jack adjusted his night-vision goggles, the world transforming into a green-tinted landscape of shadows and movement. He scanned the area, waiting for the smuggling team to arrive.

Hours passed slowly. Jack's senses were finely tuned, every rustle of leaves and distant sound heightened by the silence of his vigil. He was restless but resolute, the knowledge that this trap could be the turning point in his fight against The Colonel's network keeping him focused.

Just after midnight, Jack's patience was rewarded. A faint light bobbed in the distance, moving steadily toward the airstrip. Jack's heart rate quickened as he watched the approaching figures. They were a small team, three men, dressed in the distinctive dark uniforms of The Colonel's mercenaries. They carried flashlights and moved with purpose, their footsteps crunching softly on the gravel.

Jack tightened his grip on the rifle slung across his chest, his finger hovering near the trigger. He observed the men as they approached the decoy. They were cautious, scanning the area for any signs of trouble. The trap was set; now it was time for the final act.

The leader of the team, a burly man with a scar running down his left cheek, approached the cache. He examined the crates, his flashlight illuminating their contents. Jack held his breath, waiting for the moment when the men would fully commit to the ruse.

Suddenly, the leader's radio crackled to life. The murmur of voices was faint but audible, discussing the status of the shipment. The leader's face darkened as he listened, his eyes darting toward the forest, clearly wary of any potential ambush. Jack's instincts told him that the men were on edge, and the slightest misstep could blow the whole operation.

Jack shifted his position slightly, careful not to make a sound. He had prepared for this moment, setting up a secondary line of defense. If the men discovered the trap too early or attempted to flee, he needed to be ready. His plan included a diversion—a controlled explosion that would create chaos and cover his movements.

As the leader's team continued to inspect the cache, Jack triggered the diversion. A series of muffled explosions erupted from a nearby ridge, sending plumes of smoke and debris into the air. The men's heads snapped toward the sound, their radios crackling with frantic communications. Jack watched as they momentarily lost their composure, their focus shifting from the cache to the source of the commotion.

Taking advantage of the confusion, Jack moved swiftly. He had anticipated that the diversion would cause a temporary disarray, and he used this opportunity to position himself closer to the men. His goal was to incapacitate them without alerting the rest of The Colonel's operation.

Jack crept through the underbrush, his movements silent and precise. He reached the edge of the airstrip, where the men were scrambling to respond to the diversion. Using a combination of hand signals and low whispers, Jack coordinated his attack. He took down the first man silently, using a chokehold that rendered him unconscious before he could raise an alarm. The second man, momentarily disoriented, was taken out with a well-placed strike to the back of the head.

The leader, however, had regained his composure and was starting to realize the trap. He began to retreat, signaling his remaining men to fall back. Jack knew he had only moments before the situation escalated. He had to act quickly.

Jack pursued the leader, moving with the stealth and precision that had defined his military career. He tackled the man from behind, wrestling him to the ground. A brief struggle ensued, but Jack's superior training and physical strength quickly overwhelmed the leader. With the man subdued, Jack took his radio and earpiece, listening to the frantic messages coming through.

The messages revealed that The Colonel's network was on high alert. The men were communicating about the trapped shipment and the potential threat to their operation. Jack's heart raced as he realized that his actions had stirred a hornet's nest. The Colonel would likely intensify his efforts to secure the island and protect his interests.

Jack bound the leader's hands and feet, making sure he wouldn't escape or raise an alarm. He searched the man's pockets, finding a list of contacts and codes that could prove valuable. The information would help Jack understand the scope of The Colonel's operation and potentially identify allies or weaknesses in the network.

With the leader and his men incapacitated, Jack turned his attention to the surviving captives. He had left them hidden in a separate location, and he needed to ensure their safety. He quickly made his way back to their hiding place, where the women were waiting, their faces a mix of fear and hope.

"Stay quiet and stay put," Jack instructed as he approached. "We've had a small victory, but we're not out of danger yet."

The women nodded, their expressions tense. Jack's actions had bought them some time, but he knew that The Colonel's operation was far from defeated. The trap had been successful in drawing out some of his men, but the real challenge lay ahead. The Colonel's network was vast, and Jack's fight was only beginning.

As the first light of dawn began to filter through the trees, Jack prepared for the next phase of his plan. He had to stay one step ahead of The Colonel and his men, using every ounce of his training and ingenuity to dismantle the smuggling ring piece by piece. The island was no longer a place of quiet exile; it had become a battleground, and Jack was determined to see it through to the end.

The sun rose slowly over the horizon, casting long shadows across the island. Jack's resolve was unshakable. He had set the stage for a larger confrontation, and he was ready to face whatever came next. The Colonel's empire would not fall easily, but Jack Kincaid was prepared to fight until the very end.

Chapter 6: Betrayal Runs Deep

The relentless Pacific sun had barely begun its descent when Jack Kincaid received the message. The note, hastily scrawled on a scrap of paper, had been left in a makeshift cache—an old ammo box buried under the rotting planks of a derelict cabin. Jack, scanning the note's contents, felt a chill that had nothing to do with the encroaching evening breeze. The Colonel was extending an offer, a truce of sorts.

Jack's mind raced. A truce from The Colonel? It seemed almost absurd. But this wasn't just any offer—it was a direct communication, an invitation to parley. The note read:

"Jack, you know where to find me. I suggest you take this opportunity to discuss terms. We're not so different, you and I. Meet me at the old dock by midnight. Come alone if you value your life."

The note was signed with a simple but ominous scrawl: "The Colonel."

Jack's first reaction was a bitter laugh. The Colonel, ever the manipulator, was trying to play on Jack's past, trying to leverage their shared history to lure him into a trap. Jack had spent years dismantling every shred of connection he had to his past life. He wasn't about to walk back into it now, not without a fight.

But there was more at stake here than just his personal vendetta. If The Colonel was reaching out, it meant he was feeling the pressure. Jack had been systematically dismantling the smuggling operation with surgical precision, hitting key locations, and sabotaging their equipment. The smuggling ring was on the ropes, and now The Colonel needed a way to regain control or perhaps find a way to escape.

Jack had no intention of meeting The Colonel unprepared. If The Colonel wanted a meeting, Jack would use it as an opportunity to gain more intel, to find out what his enemy was planning, and to keep the pressure on. It was a dangerous gamble, but one that Jack was prepared to take.

By the time the sun dipped below the horizon, the island was cloaked in a shroud of darkness. Jack moved with practiced stealth, making his way to the old dock where the meeting was to take place. He approached cautiously, every sense on high alert. The old dock, once a lifeline for the island's small fishing community, was now little more than a rotting skeleton of wood and rusted metal.

The moon hung low, casting long shadows over the dilapidated structure. Jack slipped behind the remains of an old fishing boat, its hull caved in and covered with algae. He waited, hidden, for the appointed hour. His breath was steady, his heart a metronome of controlled anticipation.

As midnight approached, Jack saw movement from the direction of the island's dense jungle. A lone figure emerged, moving with a cautious but deliberate gait. It was The Colonel, unmistakable even in the gloom. His silhouette was larger than life, his movements practiced and purposeful.

Jack kept his distance, watching as The Colonel approached the center of the dock. The man was a study in contrast—wearing a pristine uniform that spoke of authority and discipline, but also of a man who had long since crossed the line from honor into corruption. Jack could see the flash of a silenced pistol strapped to The Colonel's hip, a reminder of the danger that was ever-present.

The Colonel stopped in the middle of the dock and waited, his eyes scanning the surrounding darkness. Jack didn't move, didn't make a sound. He wanted The Colonel to know he was being watched but not to be able to pinpoint his exact location.

"Jack Kincaid," The Colonel's voice broke the silence, carrying with it a blend of mockery and genuine curiosity. "I'm surprised you took me up on my offer."

Jack stepped out from his hiding place, emerging slowly into the moonlight. "You know me well enough, Colonel," he said, his voice steady and cold. "I don't back down from a challenge."

The Colonel's eyes narrowed as he took in Jack's appearance. "You've changed, Jack. The man I knew was driven by duty, honor. Now, you're just a shadow of your former self."

Jack's jaw tightened. "And you're no longer the commanding officer I respected. You've become a traitor."

The Colonel's lips curled into a smile that didn't reach his eyes. "I see you haven't lost your edge. Good. It makes this conversation more interesting."

Jack's gaze remained fixed on The Colonel, but his mind was racing. He had to keep the conversation going, find out what The Colonel was really after, and keep his own plans close to the vest.

"Why are you here, Colonel?" Jack asked. "What do you want from me?"

The Colonel's eyes gleamed with a dangerous light. "I'm here to offer you a choice, Jack. You and I have been on opposite sides for too long. It's time for a truce. I can offer you a place in this operation, a chance to join forces. We can put our skills together and control this island, control the smuggling network. We could be unstoppable."

Jack's expression remained unreadable. "And why would I ever consider joining you? You betrayed me, and you're responsible for countless lives ruined."

The Colonel's smile faded slightly. "Ah, yes. The past. I know you hold onto it tightly. But think about it, Jack. We're both men who have been cast aside by the very institutions we served. The government turned its back on you after your last mission. They made you the scapegoat, just as they did with me. We're not so different."

Jack shook his head. "You don't get to rewrite history, Colonel. I know what you did. You sold out our own, put innocent lives at risk for profit. You're no better than the criminals you're working with."

The Colonel's gaze hardened. "You still don't see the bigger picture. The government is corrupt, Jack. They use and discard people like us. I'm offering you a chance to take control, to make a real difference."

Jack's thoughts churned. The Colonel's offer was tempting in a way. It promised power, control, and a chance to strike back at the government that had betrayed him. But Jack knew better than to trust him. This was a game, and The Colonel was playing for keeps.

"No," Jack said finally. "I'm not interested in your offer. I'm here to take you down and put an end to this smuggling operation. I won't be a part of your corruption."

The Colonel's expression darkened. "A shame. I was hoping you'd see reason. But if you're determined to fight me, then we'll do this the hard way."

Jack's heart rate quickened, but he kept his expression calm. "I wouldn't have it any other way."

The Colonel's eyes gleamed with a cold, calculating intensity. "Very well. If that's your choice, then prepare for the consequences. I'll be seeing you, Jack."

With that, The Colonel turned on his heel and strode back toward the jungle, his figure gradually swallowed by the darkness. Jack watched him go, every muscle in his body tense. The meeting had confirmed what he'd suspected—The Colonel was a formidable adversary, and the stakes were higher than ever.

As The Colonel disappeared from view, Jack moved swiftly, retracing his steps back to his hideout. The conversation had given him valuable insight into The Colonel's mindset, but it had also highlighted the danger that lay ahead. The Colonel was not only a powerful enemy but a deeply dangerous one.

Jack knew he had to act quickly. The Colonel's offer had been a way to test Jack's resolve, and Jack had passed the test. But now he was even more certain of his mission. He had to dismantle the smuggling operation piece by piece, and he had to be ready for whatever The Colonel had in store for him next.

As he approached his hideout, Jack mentally prepared for the next phase of his plan. He had to stay one step ahead of The Colonel, anticipate his moves, and strike when the opportunity presented itself. The stakes were high, and the dangers were real. But Jack Kincaid was no stranger to facing the odds head-on.

With renewed determination, Jack set to work, ready to continue his relentless pursuit of justice and vengeance. The Colonel had made his move, and now it was Jack's turn to respond. The battle was far from over, and Jack was prepared to see it through to the end.

The Colonel's voice echoed in Jack's mind long after the conversation ended, lingering like the foul stench of rot that had taken over this island. The offer to make peace, to let bygones be bygones, wasn't just insulting—it was venomous. The Colonel had tried to convince him they were the same. Two soldiers, abandoned by the government they once served. But the Colonel wasn't like Jack—he was something far worse. A man who thrived in chaos, profiting from human suffering, trafficking in lives and death.

Jack sat in his makeshift cabin, the low crackle of a fire the only sound breaking the heavy silence. The women he'd rescued huddled together in the far corner, their eyes wide with fear and uncertainty. They had overheard parts of his conversation with The Colonel, and now, they too wondered which way Jack would lean. He could see it in their faces—pleading expressions, silently begging him not to turn his back on them, not to walk away.

He felt the weight of their eyes, but more than that, he felt the crushing weight of his own past bearing down on him. The guilt. The mistakes. The lives he couldn't save.

Outside, the wind howled, bending the palm trees as the first signs of another storm gathered on the horizon. Jack stood and walked to the door, opening it just enough to let the cold breeze rush in, washing over his face. He needed clarity, but the island, the ghosts, the memories—they all conspired against him, fogging his mind with doubt.

Could The Colonel be right? Was this all futile? Was he destined to be a pawn in someone else's game, no matter how hard he fought?

No.

Jack clenched his jaw, the muscles in his neck tightening as the decision took hold. He wasn't a pawn anymore. Not for The Colonel. Not for the government that had turned its back on him. He was his own man now, and he would fight for what was right—even if it meant facing the darkest parts of his past.

Jack turned back to the women. Their eyes hadn't left him. He saw the fear in them, but beneath it, there was something more. Trust. They believed he could help them. They had no one else. And as much as Jack wanted to stay out of it, to retreat into the isolation that had once been his refuge, he knew he couldn't.

"I'm going to end this," Jack said, his voice low but resolute.

One of the women, a young girl barely in her twenties, spoke up. "What happens if you fail?"

Jack paused, the question slicing through the thin veneer of confidence he was trying to project. He didn't have an answer. Failure meant they'd all be dead, or worse. But the fear of failure had never stopped him before. He had faced death more times than he could count, and every time, he had survived. This time would be no different.

"I won't fail," Jack said, his voice firm.

The girl's eyes searched his face for any sign of doubt. When she found none, she nodded, her lips trembling as she pressed them together.

"Get some rest," Jack said. "Tomorrow, we move."

He turned and headed back outside, the wind whipping against his face as he made his way toward the beach. The Colonel's men had eyes everywhere, but Jack had already started setting traps, dismantling their surveillance bit by bit. The Colonel didn't know it yet, but his days were numbered.

Jack crouched near a cluster of rocks, pulling out the crude map he'd been working on. He had been scouting the island for weeks, long before the trafficked women had washed ashore. He knew where The Colonel's men were stationed, where their supply lines were weakest, and where he could strike without drawing too much attention. The time for stealth was over, though. He needed to make his move, and he needed to do it soon.

But The Colonel had resources—men, weapons, and the backing of powerful people. Jack didn't. All he had was his training and a handful of survivors.

Jack's fingers traced the map, following the lines he had drawn, his mind calculating the odds. The Colonel's base was heavily fortified, but not impenetrable. There was a weak point—a supply dock on the far side of the island. If Jack could sabotage it, cut off The Colonel's access to his shipments, he could force the man out into the open.

The Colonel wanted to talk about betrayal, about how they were the same? Fine. Jack would show him what betrayal really looked like.

The storm hit that night. Torrential rain pounded the island, the winds tearing through the jungle with a fury that rattled even Jack. But it was the perfect cover. While The Colonel's men hunkered down, trying to weather the storm, Jack moved.

He crept through the thick underbrush, his footsteps silent against the wet ground. The rain blurred his vision, but Jack didn't need to see to know where he was going. He had memorized every inch of this island, every path, every clearing. The Colonel's men might have numbers, but Jack had the advantage of knowing the terrain better than anyone.

The dock was ahead, just beyond the next ridge. Jack stopped, crouching low as he scanned the area. Two guards. Armed, but not paying attention. They were more concerned with the storm than any potential threat. Jack smirked. They had gotten complacent. That was going to cost them.

He moved quickly, darting from shadow to shadow until he was right on top of them. The first guard didn't even see it coming. Jack's knife sliced through the rain, a clean, swift motion. The guard dropped without a sound. The second guard turned, his eyes widening in shock, but Jack was already on him. A quick punch to the throat, followed by a brutal knee to the gut. The man collapsed, gasping for air. Jack finished him off with a swift, silent strike.

The dock was clear.

Jack moved to the supply crates, quickly rummaging through them. Weapons, ammunition, food, and medical supplies. All of it would cripple The Colonel's operation if Jack could destroy it. He rigged the explosives he had fashioned from scavenged materials, setting them to a timer.

As he worked, his mind kept drifting back to The Colonel's offer. The way he had tried to paint them as two sides of the same coin. Jack had seen through it, but there was a sliver of truth buried in the Colonel's words. Both of them had been left behind, betrayed by the government they had served. But where The Colonel had chosen to embrace the darkness, Jack had spent years fighting it.

Maybe that's what made them different. Or maybe that's what made them the same. Jack couldn't afford to dwell on it now.

The timer was set. Jack moved quickly, disappearing into the night as the first explosion ripped through the dock. The ground shook beneath him as fire lit up the sky, casting a red glow over the island.

The Colonel's men would come running now, but it was too late. Jack had already vanished, melting back into the jungle like a ghost.

The next morning, Jack returned to the cabin. The women were awake, their faces pale with worry.

"What happened?" one of them asked.

"I sent The Colonel a message," Jack said, his voice cold and steady.

He didn't elaborate. They didn't need to know the details. All that mattered was that The Colonel's operation was starting to crumble.

Jack sat down, his body aching from the night's exertion. But there was no time to rest. The Colonel would retaliate. He would send more men, better trained, better equipped. And Jack knew he couldn't keep playing defense forever.

He had made his choice. Now, it was time to go on the offensive.

"We need to move," Jack said, his voice firm. "The Colonel's going to come for us. We can't stay here."

The women exchanged nervous glances, but none of them argued. They trusted Jack. They had no other choice.

Jack stood and grabbed his gear, his mind already racing through the next steps. He had bought them some time with the dock explosion, but it wouldn't last. The Colonel would regroup, and when he did, he would come at Jack with everything he had.

But Jack wasn't afraid. Not anymore. He had faced worse odds, and he had survived. The Colonel thought he could break Jack, turn him, convince him to join the darkness.

He was wrong.

Jack led the women out of the cabin and into the jungle, the weight of his choice heavy on his shoulders. But as they moved, a strange sense of peace settled over him. For the first time in years, Jack knew exactly who he was and what he needed to do.

He wasn't running anymore.

He was hunting.

Chapter 7: Island of No Escape

The sun was barely visible over the horizon when Jack Kincaid woke up. His body, used to the island's rhythm, had already adapted to the early light and the constant sound of waves crashing against the shore. He stretched, feeling the familiar ache in his muscles—a reminder of both his age and the brutal life he was living. But today, the ache was different; it was tinged with a sense of urgency.

Jack moved through his makeshift camp with practiced efficiency. He checked his weapons, ensured the traps he had set around the perimeter were still intact, and reviewed the map he had been piecing together. His attention to detail was meticulous; he could no longer afford to make mistakes.

He had been prepared for a fight, but he hadn't anticipated the sheer scale of the Colonel's operation. Every hour on the island brought new revelations about the extent of the smuggling network. Jack had seen the signs—guard posts, surveillance equipment, and a growing number of mercenaries. What he hadn't expected was the full-scale lockdown that was now taking place.

A faint sound carried over the morning breeze—a helicopter, perhaps. Jack's heart sank. The Colonel had moved swiftly. There was no doubt that the lockdown was aimed at him. The island's isolation was no longer a sanctuary; it had become a trap.

Jack stepped out of his hut and surveyed the area. The dense foliage and rocky terrain that had once been his allies now seemed to close in on him, an insidious reminder of the new threat. He could see the telltale signs of increased activity—footprints in the sand, broken branches, and disturbed earth.

The Colonel's men were thorough. They had set up roadblocks and checkpoints, cutting off the island's few access points. Jack had anticipated some resistance, but this was an entirely new level of sophistication. The Colonel was playing for keeps.

Jack quickly gathered his gear and moved towards the higher ground, where he had a better vantage point. From his perch, he could see the searchlights scanning the island and the occasional patrol moving in tight formations. They were leaving no stone unturned.

He needed to think strategically. The Colonel's forces were methodical and well-equipped. Jack's advantage lay in his knowledge of the island and his ability to use it to his advantage. But the terrain was changing rapidly. The Colonel was not just hunting him; he was reshaping the island into a fortress.

Jack crouched behind a boulder, his mind racing. He could hear the distant thrum of the helicopter, a constant reminder of the Colonel's reach. The chopper's presence meant that they were not only looking for him on the ground but also from the air. It would be impossible to avoid detection indefinitely.

He needed a plan. First, he had to stay hidden and gather as much intelligence as possible. The Colonel had made his move; now it was Jack's turn. He needed to disrupt their operation, create confusion, and find a way to neutralize the threat.

Jack decided to head towards the northern part of the island, where he had noticed fewer patrols. He moved quietly through the underbrush, every step calculated to avoid making any noise. His senses were on high alert, attuned to every sound and movement.

As he approached a clearing, Jack spotted a small group of mercenaries setting up what appeared to be a temporary command post. They were focused on their tasks, unaware of Jack's presence. He took advantage of the situation and moved closer, using the dense foliage as cover.

The Colonel's men were busy coordinating their efforts, their radios crackling with updates and orders. Jack could hear snippets of their conversation. They were searching for something—or someone—specific. Jack knew that their focus was on him, but he needed to understand their broader strategy.

From his vantage point, Jack could see the layout of their temporary camp. There were several vehicles, including an armored truck, and a number of crates and supplies. It was clear that they were preparing for a prolonged operation. This wasn't just a search-and-destroy mission; it was a full-scale lockdown.

Jack's mind raced as he formulated his plan. He needed to create chaos within the Colonel's ranks, disrupt their communications, and weaken their hold on the island. But he also had to be cautious. The Colonel's men were highly trained and heavily armed. One misstep could mean the end of him.

He decided to use his knowledge of the island's geography to his advantage. There were several old mine shafts and underground tunnels that he could use to move around undetected. These had been abandoned for years, but Jack knew them well. They provided a network of hidden paths that could help him navigate the island without being spotted.

Jack made his way towards the entrance of one of these tunnels. The entrance was well-hidden, obscured by overgrown vegetation and rocks. He had to move carefully, clearing away the debris and making sure the area was secure. Once inside, he switched on his flashlight and began to move through the dark, narrow passage.

The tunnel was damp and cold, a stark contrast to the heat of the island above. Jack followed the winding path, his footsteps echoing off the walls. He could feel the weight of the Colonel's operation pressing down on him. Every decision mattered, and every move had to be precise.

As he emerged from the tunnel on the other side of the island, Jack took a deep breath. The air was fresher here, and the noise of the Colonel's operations seemed to be muffled. He moved cautiously, keeping an eye out for any signs of patrols or security measures.

His immediate goal was to gather more intelligence. He needed to understand the full scope of the Colonel's plans and find a way to exploit any weaknesses. The Colonel was a formidable opponent, but Jack had faced worse. He was determined to use every advantage he had to turn the tide in his favor.

As the day progressed, Jack continued to scout the island, gathering information and assessing the Colonel's fortifications. The lockdown was thorough, but it wasn't impenetrable. Jack knew that with the right strategy, he could create enough disruption to shift the balance of power.

The sun was setting when Jack finally made his way back to his camp. The shadows lengthened, and the island was bathed in a dim, eerie light. He could hear the distant hum of the helicopter and the occasional shout of the Colonel's men. The lockdown was in full swing, and Jack's window of opportunity was closing.

He needed to act quickly. His plan was to strike at the heart of the Colonel's operation, disrupt their communications, and create enough confusion to slip through their defenses. It was a risky move, but it was the only way to gain the upper hand.

Jack settled in for the night, his mind focused on the task ahead. The Colonel had underestimated him, and now he was going to make him pay. The island was no longer a refuge; it was a battleground, and Jack was ready for the fight of his life.

The stakes were higher than ever, and the risks were greater. But Jack Kincaid was no stranger to danger. He had faced impossible odds before, and he had come out on top. This time would be no different. The Colonel's reign of terror was coming to an end, and Jack was determined to see it through to the end.

As the darkness enveloped the island, Jack's resolve hardened. The lockdown was just the beginning. He had a plan, and he was ready to execute it. The Colonel had made a mistake, and Jack was going to make him pay. The fight was far from over, and Jack Kincaid was just getting started.

The rain pounded relentlessly against the canopy of the dense forest, a symphony of nature's wrath that seemed to echo Jack Kincaid's internal turmoil. The storm that had battered the island had subsided, but the tempest within Jack was far from over. The Colonel's mercenaries had secured the island, trapping Jack in a perilous game of survival. With every path to escape blocked, Jack knew he had to rely on more than just his instincts; he needed allies. Yet trust was a commodity more dangerous than a loaded weapon on this island, and Jack was running out of options.

Jack crouched low behind a tangle of vines and underbrush, peering through a gap at the makeshift camp he had observed from a distance. His makeshift reconnaissance point was high in the tree line, and from here, he could see the enemy's movements with disturbing clarity. The mercenaries patrolled with an efficiency that spoke of military training, their disciplined formations a stark reminder of the threat he faced. The Colonel's men were methodical, and their presence was a constant reminder of Jack's precarious position.

He scanned the area, noting the locations of guards and supply caches. His mind worked through the tactical possibilities, calculating every potential route, every possible engagement. The realization that escape was not an option forced him to focus on another plan: forging an alliance with the survivors he had rescued. They were scared, confused, and, most importantly, their survival depended on their ability to trust one another.

In a secluded part of the island, Jack found a small, makeshift shelter where the survivors had gathered. Their expressions were a mix of fear and relief as they huddled together, trying to comprehend the gravity of their situation. Among them was Elena, the woman who had initially approached him on the beach. She had been their spokesperson, and Jack had a sense that she could be pivotal in rallying the others.

Jack emerged from the underbrush, his presence causing a brief surge of panic among the group. Elena's eyes met his, and she quickly stood to calm the others. She was a striking figure—her face marked with the fatigue of her ordeal but also a fierce resolve.

"We need to talk," Jack said, his voice carrying a weight that silenced the murmurs of the survivors. "In private."

Elena led Jack to a secluded spot away from the others, where they could converse without the risk of being overheard. The sound of the rain had dulled to a soft patter, a gentle reminder of the storm that had brought them all to this moment.

"Are they really trying to kill us?" Elena asked, her voice laced with an edge of desperation.

"Yes," Jack replied, his tone steady. "The Colonel's men have locked down the island. They're not just here to keep us in; they're here to make sure no one gets out."

Elena's expression hardened as she absorbed the gravity of Jack's words. "So what do we do?"

Jack took a deep breath. "We fight back."

A flicker of hope sparked in Elena's eyes, quickly followed by doubt. "We're outnumbered and outgunned. How can we possibly stand a chance?"

Jack didn't flinch. "We have something they don't: knowledge of the island and the will to survive. But first, we need to secure our base and prepare for the worst. I can teach you some basic tactics and how to handle weapons, but trust will be our greatest asset."

Elena nodded, a determined look in her eyes. "What do you need us to do?"

Jack laid out a plan. "We'll start by fortifying our position. I need everyone to help gather supplies—food, water, medical supplies. We'll set up a perimeter with whatever we can find. Elena, I'll need you to keep morale high and make sure everyone understands the seriousness of our situation."

Over the next few hours, Jack and the survivors worked tirelessly. They established a defensive perimeter using materials scavenged from the wreckage of the storm and remnants from the island's previous occupants. Jack demonstrated basic tactical principles—how to set up tripwires, create makeshift barricades, and use natural cover effectively. The survivors, initially hesitant, began to fall into a rhythm, their fear slowly transforming into resolve.

Despite their efforts, Jack couldn't shake the feeling that something was amiss. He observed the group closely, looking for signs of hidden agendas or potential betrayals. Trust, after all, was a dangerous game, and the stakes were higher than ever.

The following day, Jack's instincts proved correct. As he conducted a sweep of the perimeter, he noticed two of the survivors, a man named Daniel and a woman named Sarah, sneaking away from the camp. Their furtive behavior was suspicious, and Jack decided to follow them discreetly.

He trailed them through the dense forest, staying just out of sight. The terrain was treacherous, with mud-slicked ground and dense undergrowth, but Jack navigated it with ease, his senses honed from years of training. As he approached their destination, he saw Daniel and Sarah meeting with a group of armed men—mercenaries.

Jack's heart pounded as he realized the betrayal was not only a possibility but a reality. Daniel and Sarah were informing the mercenaries about the survivors' plans, trading information for promises of safety and rewards. Jack silently retreated, his mind racing through the implications of this new development.

He returned to the camp and confronted Elena privately. "We've got a problem. Two of our own are working with the enemy."

Elena's eyes widened in shock. "Who?"

"Daniel and Sarah," Jack said. "We need to act fast. If they inform The Colonel about our position, we'll be sitting ducks."

Elena nodded, her expression resolute. "What do we do?"

Jack formulated a plan. "We need to tighten security and prepare for an immediate assault. I'll handle the traitors. The rest of you focus on reinforcing our defenses. We can't afford to be caught off guard."

As Jack prepared to deal with the traitors, he was acutely aware of the delicate balance he had to maintain. He needed to ensure the survivors were ready for the impending attack while simultaneously dealing with the internal threat. The tension in the camp was palpable, a mix of fear, anger, and determination.

Jack's mind was focused, his training taking over. He moved with purpose, setting up additional defenses and coordinating with Elena to keep the survivors' spirits up. The impending threat from both within and outside the camp made every moment crucial.

In the depths of the island's foliage, Jack confronted Daniel and Sarah. The confrontation was swift and decisive. Jack's training allowed him to neutralize the threat without causing unnecessary harm. He ensured that Daniel and Sarah would be unable to compromise their position further, then made his way back to the camp.

The atmosphere was tense as Jack returned. Elena and the others had been busy reinforcing their defenses, their preparations a testament to their growing determination. Jack quickly briefed them on the situation.

"The traitors are dealt with," Jack said, his voice steady. "We're facing a coordinated attack. Expect an assault within the next few hours. We need to be ready."

The survivors responded with a mix of fear and resolve. They had faced unimaginable horrors and were now faced with a new challenge: defending their temporary refuge against a ruthless enemy. Jack's leadership was critical, and he knew that their survival hinged on their ability to work together.

As night fell, the tension in the camp was palpable. Jack and the survivors took their positions, their makeshift defenses ready for the imminent assault. Jack's mind raced through potential scenarios, preparing himself for the brutal conflict that was about to unfold.

The island, once a place of isolation and escape, had become a battleground. Jack had traded his solitude for a fight for survival, and as he looked out over the darkened landscape, he knew that the coming hours would test every ounce of his resolve and skill. The battle for the island was about to begin, and Jack was determined to emerge victorious, no matter the cost.

In the darkness of the night, the sound of approaching footsteps and the distant murmur of voices signaled the start of the assault. Jack and the survivors braced themselves for the fight of their lives, their trust in each other their only hope of surviving the onslaught. The fate of the island, and perhaps their lives, rested on their ability to withstand the coming storm.

Chapter 8: Breaking Point

Jack Kincaid crouched low behind a large, gnarled tree trunk, its bark thick and weathered by countless seasons. The remnants of a previous skirmish—a discarded rifle, a torn combat vest—lay scattered around him. His breathing was controlled, slow, every muscle tensed for the inevitable fight. The island, once a refuge, had transformed into a battleground.

The relentless drone of helicopters in the distance marked the beginning of a new chapter in his war against The Colonel. The smuggler's mercenaries had initiated a full-scale assault. Jack had anticipated this escalation, but the reality of it was overwhelming. The Colonel had grown impatient with Jack's interference, and now he intended to crush him with sheer force.

From his vantage point, Jack surveyed the scene unfolding below. The dense foliage had been set ablaze, sending plumes of thick smoke into the sky. The mercenaries had moved swiftly, establishing a perimeter around the makeshift hideout where Jack and his allies were entrenched. The air was heavy with the acrid smell of burning wood and gunpowder. The once serene island was now a tableau of chaos.

Jack's small group of allies—survivors from the smuggling operations and local islanders—were scattered throughout the hideout, using the natural terrain to their advantage. They had fortified their position as best they could, constructing barriers from fallen trees and constructing defensive lines with whatever materials they could scavenge. But even their best efforts seemed flimsy in the face of the Colonel's might.

Jack had no illusions about the scale of the Colonel's resources. The Colonel had been preparing for a confrontation like this, amassing a force capable of overwhelming any resistance. Jack's guerrilla tactics had disrupted the smuggling operation, but now the full brunt of The Colonel's vengeance was being unleashed.

As he watched, Jack spotted movement—a squad of mercenaries advancing through the smoke, their black uniforms stark against the gray haze. They were heavily armed, their weapons glinting in the flickering light of the fires. Jack's eyes narrowed as he recognized their formation: they were advancing methodically, cutting off any potential escape routes and preparing to breach the hideout.

Jack needed a plan. He had prepared for an assault, but the scale of this attack demanded something more. He reached for his radio, the small device crackling to life as he spoke in low, urgent tones. "Listen up. They're closing in. We need to fortify our defenses and prepare for a counterattack. Conserve ammunition and focus on the most significant threats."

The response was a series of terse acknowledgments. Jack turned his attention to the makeshift barricades. His allies worked furiously, reinforcing their positions. The sense of urgency was palpable, each person driven by the fear of imminent destruction. Jack moved among them, offering brief words of encouragement and tactical advice. His presence was a beacon of calm amidst the chaos, a reminder that they were not alone.

In the distance, the sound of explosions punctuated the oppressive silence. The Colonel's forces had begun their assault, lobbing grenades and mortars into the area surrounding the hideout. The ground shook with each blast, sending tremors through the makeshift barricades and sending plumes of dust and debris into the air.

Jack ducked as shrapnel whizzed past him, his mind working furiously to assess the situation. He knew that the assault was not just about overwhelming them; it was also a psychological tactic designed to break their will. The Colonel was not just fighting to eliminate Jack; he was fighting to demoralize and destroy everything Jack had built.

Jack's eyes caught movement to his right. A small group of mercenaries was making a push through a gap in the defenses. Without hesitation, Jack grabbed a nearby rifle and moved into position. His training kicked in, and he fired precise shots, targeting the mercenaries as they attempted to breach the hideout. The first few fell quickly, but the remaining mercenaries took cover and began returning fire.

The firefight intensified, the air filled with the deafening roar of gunfire and the acrid stench of smoke. Jack's allies were engaged in a desperate struggle, their voices rising in a cacophony of commands and cries for help. The Colonel's mercenaries were relentless, pushing forward with a brutality that matched their numbers.

Jack's mind raced as he directed his allies, moving between positions and coordinating their defense. He could see the stress and exhaustion etched on their faces, the strain of the battle taking its toll. But he also saw determination—an unwavering resolve to fight back, to protect their home and their lives.

As the battle raged on, Jack caught sight of a new threat: a pair of armored vehicles approaching from the south. The Colonel had clearly anticipated a prolonged fight and had brought in heavy support. The vehicles were equipped with mounted machine guns, and their appearance signaled a shift in the battle's dynamics.

Jack knew that the armored vehicles would be a game-changer. They could easily overwhelm their defenses and force a breakthrough. He grabbed his radio again, his voice steady despite the chaos. "We've got armored vehicles incoming. Focus fire on the vehicles. Use explosives if you have them. We can't let them breach our lines."

The response was immediate. Jack's allies scrambled to prepare their remaining resources, setting up makeshift traps and positioning themselves to engage the armored vehicles. Jack took up a position with a high-powered rifle, his eyes scanning the approaching vehicles.

The first vehicle reached the edge of the hideout's perimeter, its machine gun spitting a hail of bullets into the defensive lines. Jack took aim, firing at the vehicle's vulnerable spots. His shots struck true, damaging the vehicle's engine and causing it to shudder and slow. But the second vehicle continued its advance, its machine gun blazing.

Jack's allies responded with a barrage of fire, their combined efforts forcing the second vehicle to retreat. The battle was far from over, but the immediate threat of the armored vehicles had been temporarily neutralized.

Jack took a moment to regroup, assessing the damage and the casualties. His allies were exhausted, their numbers thinning under the relentless assault. Jack knew they couldn't hold out forever. The Colonel's forces were well-organized and relentless, and the prolonged fight was taking its toll.

In the midst of the chaos, Jack spotted a familiar figure—a woman from the group of trafficked survivors. She was moving through the battlefield, her face a mask of fear and determination. Jack's heart sank as he realized she was carrying a bundle of supplies—a small but critical stockpile of ammunition and medical supplies.

The woman made her way to Jack, her eyes filled with a desperate hope. "We need more time," she said, her voice barely audible over the din of battle. "There are more supplies coming. We just need to hold out."

Jack nodded, taking the supplies from her. He knew that they needed every advantage they could get. The battle was far from over, and the Colonel's forces were closing in. Jack turned his attention back to the fight, his mind focused on finding a way to turn the tide.

The sun was beginning to set, casting long shadows over the battlefield. The fading light did little to ease the intensity of the fight, the darkness only adding to the sense of foreboding. Jack knew that nightfall would bring its own set of challenges, making it even more difficult to hold their position.

Jack's radio crackled to life again. "We've got a situation. There's movement on the eastern flank. It looks like they're preparing for another push."

Jack's heart sank. The Colonel's forces were not letting up. He knew that this next push could be the final attempt to break through their defenses. He gathered his allies, giving them a brief but urgent pep talk. "This is it. We hold this line or we lose everything. Stay focused, stay sharp. We can't afford to falter now."

The tension was palpable as they prepared for the next wave of the assault. Jack took up his position, his rifle steady in his hands. The Colonel's forces were closing in, their advance slow but relentless. The smoke and debris obscured their movements, but Jack could see enough to know that they were preparing for a full-scale breach.

As the enemy approached, Jack's allies opened fire, their combined efforts creating a wall of resistance. The sound of gunfire was deafening, the flashes of muzzle fire lighting up the darkness. Jack fought alongside them, his movements precise and deliberate. He could feel the weight of the battle bearing down on him, the exhaustion and adrenaline blending into a single, unrelenting force.

The Colonel's forces were determined, their advance relentless. They pushed forward with a grim determination, their numbers overwhelming. Jack could see the determination in their eyes, the same kind of resolve that drove him to fight. He knew that they were fighting for their lives, and the stakes were higher than ever.

In the midst of the battle, Jack spotted a figure in the distance—The Colonel. He was overseeing the assault from a vantage point, his presence a stark reminder of the personal vendetta driving the conflict. Jack's eyes narrowed as he took aim, his mind focused on the possibility of ending this conflict once and for all.

But before he could take the shot, a burst of gunfire erupted nearby, forcing him to take cover. The Colonel's forces were closing in, their numbers overwhelming. Jack's allies fought bravely, their resistance a testament to their determination.

As the battle raged on, Jack realized that the tide of the fight was shifting. The Colonel's forces were pressing harder, their assault more coordinated. Jack knew that they had to hold their ground, but the pressure was mounting. Every second counted, every decision could be the difference between victory and defeat.

Jack's mind raced as he fought, his focus on the immediate threats. The battle was taking its toll, the exhaustion and stress pushing him to his limits. But he knew that giving up was not an option. He had to hold the line, to protect the survivors and stop The Colonel's forces.

The sound of gunfire was deafening, the air thick with smoke and debris. Jack fought with every ounce of strength he had, his movements precise and deliberate. The battle was far from over, and the outcome was uncertain. But Jack was determined to see it through, to fight until the very end.

As the night wore on, the battle reached its peak. The Colonel's forces were relentless, their assault unyielding. Jack and his allies fought with a fierce determination, their resistance a testament to their resolve. The outcome of the battle was still uncertain, but Jack knew that they had to hold their ground.

Jack took a deep breath, his focus sharp and unwavering. The battle was reaching its climax, and the stakes were higher than ever. He fought alongside his allies, their combined efforts creating a wall of resistance against the Colonel's forces.

The sound of gunfire continued to fill the air, the flashes of muzzle fire lighting up the darkness. Jack's mind was focused on the immediate threats, his movements precise and deliberate. The battle was far from over, but Jack was determined to see it through, to fight until the very end.

As the night wore on, the outcome of the battle remained uncertain. The Colonel's forces were closing in, their assault relentless. Jack knew that every second counted, every decision could be the difference between victory and defeat. He fought with every ounce of strength he had, his determination unyielding.

The battle reached its peak, the air thick with smoke and debris. Jack and his allies fought with a fierce resolve, their resistance a testament to their will. The outcome of the battle was still unknown, but Jack knew that they had to hold their ground.

Jack Kincaid was no stranger to chaos, but as he took stock of the battle unfolding around him, he couldn't help but feel a pang of disbelief. The Colonel had escalated the situation beyond anything Jack had anticipated. What had started as a skirmish was now a full-blown assault. The dense forest that had once offered cover was now a battleground, and every corner of the island seemed to be alive with the sounds of war.

Jack moved with purpose, his every sense attuned to the chaos. His survival instincts, honed by years of military service, kicked in. He navigated the treacherous terrain with precision, firing at the advancing enemy while keeping a wary eye on the movement of his allies. His hands were steady, his aim true, but the weight of the battle was beginning to take its toll.

The Colonel's forces were relentless. The sheer number of enemy combatants was overwhelming. They stormed the island in waves, their firepower relentless and unyielding. Jack and his allies fought fiercely, their makeshift defenses holding up under intense pressure. But Jack knew that they couldn't sustain this for long. They were outnumbered and outgunned.

Amidst the barrage of gunfire, Jack's mind raced. He knew that if they were to survive this, they needed to understand their enemy's true intentions. He had an inkling that there was more at stake than just a power struggle. The Colonel's tactics were too calculated, his attacks too coordinated. There had to be a deeper strategy behind the chaos.

Jack's opportunity came when he managed to push through a breach in the enemy lines. He fought his way into a small, partially destroyed building that had once served as a storage facility. The building's interior was dark and filled with debris, but Jack's instincts told him it was worth investigating. The Colonel's secret might be hidden somewhere in this ruin.

Breathing heavily, Jack took a moment to regroup. He scanned the room, his eyes catching on a small desk shoved into a corner. It looked untouched, almost out of place amidst the wreckage. With a grim determination, Jack approached the desk and began to search its contents.

Drawers were filled with various papers and documents, many of which had been hastily shoved aside. Jack sifted through them, looking for anything that might shed light on The Colonel's plans. His fingers brushed against a leather-bound folder, its cover marked with a symbol that looked vaguely familiar.

Jack opened the folder carefully, his heart racing. Inside, he found a series of documents detailing the smuggling operation in intricate detail. Maps of the island showed various hidden caches and escape routes. There were records of shipments, lists of names, and a disturbing number of connections to high-level government officials.

Jack's eyes widened as he flipped through the documents. The revelations were staggering. The Colonel was not just a rogue operative; he was a key player in a much larger, more dangerous game. The smuggling operation was being funded and protected by powerful figures in the government. The Colonel's reach extended far beyond the island, touching the highest echelons of power.

Jack's mind raced as he absorbed the implications. The scale of the operation was much larger than he had imagined. The Colonel was not just running a criminal enterprise; he was part of a network of corruption that spanned continents. The government officials involved were ensuring that The Colonel's activities remained hidden, providing him with the resources and protection needed to operate with impunity.

As Jack processed the information, he heard the distant sound of gunfire growing louder. The battle was intensifying, and Jack knew he had to act quickly. He gathered the documents and tucked them into his backpack, his thoughts already turning to how he could use this information to turn the tide of the battle.

He emerged from the building and made his way back to the front lines, where the fight was reaching its peak. The scene was chaotic, with flashes of gunfire illuminating the darkness and the acrid smell of smoke hanging heavy in the air. Jack's allies were holding their own, but they were clearly exhausted and in desperate need of reinforcements.

Jack took up position beside them, his presence a much-needed boost. He shouted instructions, directing his allies to reinforce weak points in their defenses and to focus on taking out key enemy positions. Despite the dire circumstances, Jack's tactical mind was in overdrive, using every advantage he could find to turn the battle in their favor.

The battle raged on, with both sides locked in a brutal, unrelenting struggle. Jack's mind was constantly shifting between the immediate threats and the larger picture. The Colonel's secret was now a critical piece of the puzzle, and Jack knew that exposing it could change the course of the fight.

As the night wore on, the battle began to shift. Jack's strategies and tactics started to make a difference. The Colonel's forces, though still formidable, were beginning to show signs of faltering. Jack could see the frustration and confusion on their faces, and he knew that the tide was slowly turning.

But even as he pressed his advantage, Jack remained acutely aware of the risks. The Colonel's men were not just ordinary soldiers; they were well-trained and highly motivated. Every move Jack made had to be precise, every action carefully calculated. One mistake could cost him and his allies everything.

The hours dragged on, the battle showing no signs of letting up. Jack's exhaustion was palpable, but his resolve remained unshaken. The Colonel's secret was now a driving force, propelling him forward through the chaos and carnage.

As dawn approached, the first light of morning began to filter through the smoke and debris. The battle was still raging, but Jack could see that the enemy was beginning to retreat. The Colonel's forces were withdrawing, their assault losing its intensity.

Jack knew that the battle was far from over. The Colonel would not give up easily, and there were still many challenges ahead. But for now, the immediate threat had been pushed back. Jack's focus was on regrouping and preparing for the next phase of the fight.

He looked around at his allies, their faces etched with exhaustion and determination. They had fought bravely, and their efforts had made a significant difference. Jack knew that they would need to rest and regroup, but there was no time for complacency.

With the documents in hand and a clearer understanding of The Colonel's operation, Jack knew that he had a crucial advantage. The secret he had uncovered was a powerful tool, one that could help him expose the corruption and dismantle the smuggling ring. But he also knew that the fight was far from over, and there were still many battles left to be fought.

As the sun rose over the island, casting a new light on the ravaged landscape, Jack Kincaid stood firm, ready to face whatever challenges lay ahead. The battle for the island was far from finished, but with the Colonel's secret now in his possession, Jack was more determined than ever to see it through to the end.

Chapter 9: Final Countdown

The storm had passed, leaving behind a sky bruised and scarred by the fury of nature. Jack Kincaid stood on the edge of a jagged cliff, staring out at the tumultuous ocean. The waves crashed violently against the rocks below, their spray mingling with the rain that still drizzled from the heavy clouds. The island, which had once been his sanctuary, was now a battleground of deception and bloodshed. The sight was a grim reminder of the stakes at hand.

Jack had just received intelligence from one of the survivors he had managed to rescue. The Colonel, the man who had once been his commanding officer, was planning to flee the island with a shipment of weapons and captives. It was a critical moment—Jack knew that if he failed to stop The Colonel, the smuggling ring would vanish into the ether, and countless lives would be at risk.

He turned away from the cliff and headed back to the makeshift command center he and the survivors had set up in an abandoned bunker. The air inside was thick with tension, a palpable mix of fear and determination. The survivors—women who had been trafficked, along with a few locals who had been coerced into assisting The Colonel—were gathered around a map spread out on a table. Their faces were drawn, but there was a steely resolve in their eyes.

Jack stepped into the room, his presence drawing their attention. He could see the strain in their faces, a reflection of the situation's gravity. He cleared his throat, trying to maintain an air of calm despite the gnawing urgency.

"We've got a problem," he began, his voice steady but urgent. "The Colonel is making his move. We've got confirmation that he's planning to leave the island with a shipment of weapons and captives. If we don't stop him, he'll disappear, and we'll lose our chance to dismantle this operation once and for all."

A murmur of concern swept through the room. Jack knew that time was not on their side. The Colonel had proven to be a formidable adversary, and the clock was ticking down to what could be their final confrontation.

"We need to act fast," Jack continued, pulling the map closer to him. "Here's what we know. The Colonel's stronghold is located in the southern part of the island. We've managed to gather intel that indicates he's planning to transport the shipment through a series of hidden tunnels leading to a secluded dock on the western shore."

He pointed to the map, highlighting the key locations. The survivors leaned in, their eyes fixed on the lines and markings that represented their best hope of stopping the smuggling ring.

"We'll split into two groups," Jack said, outlining his plan. "Group one will create a diversion at the stronghold to draw the Colonel's attention away from the tunnels. Group two will move in to intercept the shipment before it reaches the dock."

He paused, gauging the reaction of his team. They were clearly scared but determined. Jack knew that the mission ahead was dangerous, but it was their only chance to stop The Colonel and put an end to the smuggling operation.

"Any questions?" Jack asked, his gaze sweeping over the room.

A woman named Elena, one of the survivors who had proven to be resourceful, raised her hand. "What about the guards? The Colonel's men will be heavily armed and ready for a fight."

Jack nodded. "We've got intel on their patrol routes and weaknesses. We'll use guerrilla tactics to take them out silently and avoid unnecessary confrontation. The element of surprise will be our greatest advantage."

He turned to face the locals, who had been coerced into assisting The Colonel. They had proven their loyalty by aiding Jack in previous operations, but he knew their motivation was driven by fear as much as anything else.

"Are you all prepared for what's coming?" Jack asked them. "This is our chance to end this nightmare, but it's going to be tough."

A grizzled man named Raul, who had shown a surprising amount of bravery, stepped forward. "We're with you, Kincaid. We know what's at stake."

Jack appreciated the support but knew the path ahead was fraught with peril. He began to organize the groups, assigning specific roles and responsibilities. The plan was simple yet perilous: create chaos to disrupt The Colonel's plans and then strike decisively before he could escape.

As the teams prepared to move out, Jack took a moment to check his gear. His tactical vest was packed with ammunition, medical supplies, and other essentials. His trusted M4 rifle was slung across his back, and his sidearm was holstered at his hip. He felt the familiar weight of responsibility settle on his shoulders, a burden he had grown accustomed to but never fully accepted.

The plan was to launch the diversion just after nightfall. The cover of darkness would provide them with the best chance of slipping past The Colonel's defenses. Jack glanced at his watch, noting the time. There was no room for delay. Every second counted.

As the sun dipped below the horizon, painting the sky in shades of red and orange, Jack's team moved into position. The first group headed towards the stronghold, while Jack and his team made their way towards the tunnels. The island was eerily quiet, the only sounds being the rustling of leaves and the occasional call of a distant bird.

Jack led his group through the dense underbrush, carefully avoiding the patrols he knew would be on high alert. He communicated with his team using hand signals, a silent agreement that they would stick to the plan and remain as undetected as possible.

They reached the entrance to the tunnels, hidden behind a thick curtain of vines and foliage. Jack signaled for the team to halt and assessed the area. The entrance was well concealed, but he had been able to gather enough information to know its exact location.

He pushed aside the vines and peered into the darkness. The tunnel stretched ahead, its depths swallowed by shadows.

Jack knew that getting through would be a challenge, but the success of the mission depended on their ability to reach the dock before The Colonel's shipment did.

"Stay alert," Jack whispered to his team. "We're about to enter enemy territory. Move fast and stay quiet."

The team nodded in understanding and followed Jack into the tunnel. The air was damp and musty, the walls lined with moisture that dripped steadily onto the floor. Jack led the way, using a small flashlight to illuminate the path ahead. The tunnel was narrow, forcing them to move in single file. The oppressive darkness seemed to close in around them, adding to the tension of the moment.

As they advanced through the tunnel, Jack's mind raced with thoughts of the confrontation to come. The Colonel was a dangerous adversary, and the stakes were higher than ever. Failure was not an option—too many lives depended on their success.

After what felt like an eternity, they emerged from the tunnel and found themselves at the edge of the dock. The area was poorly lit, with only a few flickering lamps casting eerie shadows over the crates and barrels that lined the dock. Jack could see the silhouettes of armed guards patrolling the area, their movements deliberate and cautious.

Jack and his team took cover behind a stack of crates, their breathing shallow and their senses heightened. They needed to move quickly and quietly to ensure that The Colonel's shipment did not escape.

He checked his watch again, noting the time. The diversion at the stronghold should be in full swing by now. The Colonel would be preoccupied, giving Jack and his team the best chance to intercept the shipment.

Jack's plan was to disable the guards silently and then secure the area around the dock. They had to be prepared for anything, and he knew that The Colonel's men would not take kindly to their intrusion.

The team began to move into position, each member taking out a guard with precision and efficiency. Jack felt a surge of adrenaline as they worked, knowing that the success of their mission depended on their ability to remain unseen and strike with precision.

As the last guard fell, Jack signaled for his team to advance. They quickly took control of the dock, ensuring that no one could escape. The crates and barrels were examined, revealing a shipment of weapons and supplies—evidence of The Colonel's illegal activities.

Jack felt a grim satisfaction as he prepared to destroy the evidence, knowing that this was a crucial step in dismantling the smuggling ring. But he also knew that time was running out. The Colonel was still out there, and he would not rest until he had dealt with him.

With the shipment secured and the area under control, Jack made a final check of the surroundings. The stronghold diversion had gone off as planned, and The Colonel's forces were in disarray. But the battle was far from over.

Jack and his team had accomplished their primary objective, but the real challenge lay ahead. They needed to ensure that The Colonel could not escape and that the smuggling ring would be brought to justice. As he prepared for the next phase of their operation, Jack knew that the final confrontation was looming, and the outcome would determine the fate of the island and its people.

The clock was ticking, and Jack Kincaid was ready to see the mission through to its end. The Colonel's days were numbered, and Jack was determined to bring him to justice, no matter the cost.

The storm had passed, leaving behind a battered and exhausted island. The once-unyielding landscape was now a mix of shattered trees and eroded shoreline. For Jack Kincaid, the storm's aftermath was not merely a disruption but a crucial time to act. He had been monitoring the Colonel's movements for weeks, piecing together a puzzle of corruption and cruelty that had ensnared countless lives.

Jack's solitary preparation was disrupted by the arrival of the Colonel's mercenaries, a contingent of heavily armed men now patrolling the island with heightened vigilance. Every patrol and checkpoint was meticulously timed and synchronized. The Colonel's men were on high alert, likely due to the recent setbacks Jack had inflicted upon them. To get past their defenses, Jack needed a plan that was as audacious as it was precise.

Jack crouched behind a ridge overlooking the Colonel's compound, the skeletal remains of an old logging camp now converted into a fortress. From this vantage point, he could see the compound's layout—a mix of shipping containers, makeshift barricades, and guard towers. The Colonel's operation had evolved from a hidden base into a fortified stronghold, brimming with contraband and secrets.

As the sun dipped below the horizon, Jack began his approach. The fading light was both an ally and an adversary.

It offered cover but also made navigation tricky. He wore dark, practical clothing and carried only essential gear: a silenced pistol, a combat knife, and a few smoke grenades. His eyes were sharp, constantly scanning for movement or unexpected obstacles.

Using his knowledge of the island's terrain, Jack maneuvered silently through the dense forest, his footsteps muffled by the thick undergrowth. Every sense was on high alert, every sound amplified in the oppressive silence. He had mapped out the patrol routes, but the Colonel's recent security enhancements had made predicting movements more difficult.

Jack approached the eastern perimeter of the compound, a less guarded area that had once been used for storing logs but was now a vulnerable point in the Colonel's defenses. He spotted the weak spot—a section of fencing where the wire had been partially torn away, likely from the storm. Jack could exploit this gap to slip into the compound unnoticed.

As he eased through the torn fencing, Jack found himself in the shadow of one of the shipping containers. He took a moment to assess the surroundings, noting the positions of the guards and the layout of the internal structures. The compound was a hive of activity, with mercenaries moving about and the hum of generators providing a constant background noise. Jack's plan hinged on getting close enough to disrupt the Colonel's operations without being detected.

His first move was to eliminate the most immediate threat—a guard stationed near the main entrance. Jack silently approached, his movements fluid and deliberate. The guard, engrossed in checking his equipment, was unaware of Jack's presence until it was too late. Jack's knife flashed in the dim light, and the guard crumpled silently to the ground.

With the guard out of the way, Jack moved swiftly towards the control room of the compound. This was where the Colonel's operations were coordinated, and where valuable information and equipment were likely stored. As he navigated the maze of containers and makeshift barricades, Jack encountered more mercenaries. Each confrontation was a calculated risk, but Jack's experience and training allowed him to handle each threat with precision.

The control room was heavily guarded, but Jack had anticipated this. He used a smoke grenade to create a diversion, filling the immediate area with thick, opaque smoke. The mercenaries inside, disoriented and unable to see, scrambled to assess the situation. Jack used the confusion to slip inside, silently neutralizing any guards in his path.

Inside the control room, Jack found a large array of surveillance monitors and communication equipment. He quickly located the main server and began to search for any files or information that could help him understand the scope of the Colonel's plans. His heart raced as he scanned through encrypted files and classified documents.

Among the data, Jack discovered something that made his blood run cold—a detailed plan for an imminent evacuation. The Colonel was preparing to move a massive shipment of weapons and human cargo off the island, using a remote dock hidden from prying eyes. This shipment was critical; if it left, it would not only secure the Colonel's power but also entrench the criminal network's grip on the region.

Jack's mind raced as he formulated a plan to intercept the shipment. He needed to disrupt the evacuation and ensure that the Colonel's operation was brought to a halt. He set up explosives around the control room, intending to destroy the evidence and slow down the Colonel's plans. As he prepared to leave, Jack's thoughts were interrupted by the sound of approaching footsteps.

Jack had to move quickly. He slipped out of the control room and made his way towards the dock. The path was fraught with danger, with more mercenaries patrolling the area and heightened security measures. Jack's strategy was to create further diversions, drawing attention away from the dock while he executed his primary objective.

Using a combination of stealth and tactical sabotage, Jack successfully reached the dock. The area was bustling with activity as the Colonel's men prepared for the evacuation. The sight of the crates being loaded onto boats and the captives being herded together fueled Jack's determination. He had to act now.

Jack set up a series of strategically placed explosives around the dock, aiming to cause maximum disruption. With a deep breath, he triggered the explosions, creating chaos and confusion among the mercenaries. As the dock erupted in flames and debris, Jack used the ensuing chaos to free the captives and eliminate any remaining threats.

The battle at the dock was intense. Jack fought with a mix of fierce determination and tactical precision. Each movement was calculated, each action deliberate. He knew that the success of this mission depended on his ability to remain focused and adaptable.

As the fire raged and the dock was engulfed in flames, Jack fought his way through the chaos, ensuring that all the captives were safely evacuated. The mission was far from over, but Jack had achieved a critical victory. The Colonel's plans for evacuation had been thwarted, and the compound's operations were in disarray.

With the dock secured and the captives freed, Jack prepared for the next phase of his mission: infiltrating the heart of the Colonel's operation. He had gained valuable information and disrupted key elements of the smuggling network, but the ultimate confrontation with the Colonel awaited. Jack knew that he was now deeper into the lion's den than ever before, and the final showdown was imminent.

As the sun began to rise over the burning dock, Jack prepared to face the challenges that lay ahead. The Colonel was a formidable adversary, and the stakes were higher than ever. With determination and a steely resolve, Jack Kincaid braced himself for the final confrontation that would determine the fate of the island and the lives of countless individuals.

Chapter 10: The Colonel Confronted

Jack Kincaid's heart pounded in his chest as he approached the compound, the oppressive heat of the island pressing down on him like a physical weight. He had spent days meticulously planning his assault on The Colonel's stronghold, knowing that this was his last chance to end the smuggling operation once and for all. His resolve was unwavering, even as the ghosts of his past continued to haunt him.

The stronghold was a fortress of steel and concrete, nestled deep within the island's dense jungle. The outer perimeter was heavily guarded, and Jack knew that getting past the initial defenses would be no easy task. He had spent hours studying the compound's layout, mapping out the patrol routes and identifying weak points in the security.

Jack's mind raced as he approached the perimeter fence. He was dressed in dark, tactical gear, blending seamlessly into the shadows. His plan was simple yet risky: infiltrate the compound, locate The Colonel, and end this nightmare. The problem was that The Colonel was a ghost—an elusive figure who had a knack for slipping through the fingers of those who sought him. Jack had to be both cunning and ruthless if he hoped to succeed.

As Jack slipped through the dense undergrowth, he could hear the distant hum of generators and the occasional burst of laughter from the guards stationed around the compound. The sound of heavy machinery and the smell of diesel fuel filled the air. Jack moved with the precision of a predator, his every step calculated and deliberate.

He reached the outer fence, a formidable barrier of razor wire and electrified barriers. Jack had anticipated this and had brought with him a cutting torch, which he used to carefully slice through the wire. The sparks flew, and Jack's heart raced as he worked quickly to avoid detection. The compound was a hive of activity, and he couldn't afford to be spotted.

Once the fence was breached, Jack crawled through the gap and into the compound. The interior was a maze of concrete walls and steel structures, with a series of watchtowers and guard posts strategically placed to monitor the area. Jack moved stealthily, sticking to the shadows and avoiding the patrols.

He navigated through the compound, his eyes scanning for any sign of The Colonel. The layout was just as he had studied, and he soon found himself in a central control room filled with monitors displaying various parts of the compound. Jack's heart sank as he saw the feeds—The Colonel was still here, and he was surrounded by a cadre of heavily armed mercenaries.

Jack took a deep breath and activated his comms, speaking softly into the radio. "I'm in. I have eyes on The Colonel. He's in the control room with several guards. I'll need a diversion to get close."

The voice on the other end was calm and reassuring. "Copy that, Jack. We're setting up a diversion now. Stay sharp and be ready."

Jack's plan hinged on the diversion. He needed to create chaos to draw the guards away from The Colonel and give himself a chance to strike. He moved to a vantage point, positioning himself where he could observe the control room and the surrounding area.

Moments later, a series of explosions rocked the compound. The sound of gunfire and shouting filled the air as Jack's allies launched their attack. The diversion was working—the guards in the control room scrambled to respond to the threat, leaving The Colonel momentarily exposed.

Jack seized the opportunity and made his move. He darted through the compound, his movements swift and silent. He avoided the main corridors, instead taking a series of back passages and maintenance tunnels that led him closer to The Colonel's location.

As he approached the control room, Jack's heart pounded in his chest. He knew that this was the moment he had been waiting for—a chance to confront the man who had betrayed him and caused so much suffering. His anger and determination were palpable, fueling his every action.

Jack reached the control room's entrance and peered inside. The Colonel was seated at a large desk, surrounded by monitors and maps. His face was as cold and calculating as ever, but Jack could see the flicker of concern in his eyes as he tried to regain control of the situation.

With a deep breath, Jack pushed through the door and into the control room. The Colonel's head snapped up, and his eyes widened in surprise. "Kincaid," he said, his voice a mixture of shock and disdain. "I should have known you'd come crawling back."

The Colonel's guards quickly drew their weapons, but Jack was faster. He moved with lethal efficiency, taking out the guards with a combination of precise shots and well-placed hand-to-hand combat. The control room was soon filled with the sounds of gunfire and the cries of the dying.

The Colonel tried to escape, but Jack was relentless. He pursued him through the compound, their paths intersecting in a series of narrow hallways and hidden passages. The Colonel was surprisingly agile for a man of his age, but Jack's determination and skill gave him the edge.

Finally, they reached a large, open chamber—a makeshift command center that The Colonel had set up for his operation. The room was filled with maps, communication equipment, and crates of illicit goods. The Colonel turned to face Jack, his expression a mixture of anger and resignation.

"You're a fool, Kincaid," The Colonel sneered. "You think you can stop me? You think you're the hero in this story? You're nothing but a washed-up has-been."

Jack's eyes burned with anger. "You betrayed me. You betrayed everyone who trusted you. You're going to pay for everything you've done."

The two men faced off, their tension palpable. The Colonel moved with a practiced grace, but Jack was relentless. The fight was brutal, each man using their skills and knowledge of combat to their advantage. The room became a battleground, filled with the sounds of clashing metal and shattering glass.

Jack's rage fueled his every move. He wasn't just fighting for himself; he was fighting for the victims, for the people who had suffered because of The Colonel's actions. His strikes were precise and devastating, each one bringing him closer to his goal.

As the battle raged on, Jack managed to corner The Colonel. The two men stood face-to-face, their breaths coming in ragged gasps. Jack's eyes were locked on The Colonel's, his anger and determination clear.

"You're finished," Jack said, his voice low and fierce. "It's over."

The Colonel's eyes narrowed. "You think you've won? You're nothing. You're a pawn in a game you don't understand."

With a final, powerful strike, Jack brought The Colonel to the ground. The fight was over, but the victory felt hollow. As The Colonel lay defeated, Jack realized that he had only scratched the surface of a much larger conspiracy. The Colonel had been a pawn in a larger scheme, and the true extent of the corruption and betrayal was yet to be uncovered.

Jack's mind raced as he surveyed the aftermath of the battle. The control room was in shambles, the once-pristine equipment now broken and scattered. The Colonel's reign of terror was over, but Jack knew that the fight was far from finished. The powerful figures who had supported The Colonel were still out there, and they would stop at nothing to protect their interests.

Jack took a deep breath, his mind already shifting to the next phase of his mission. He had to uncover the full extent of the conspiracy and ensure that those responsible for the smuggling operation were brought to justice. The battle was over, but the war was just beginning.

The sun was setting, casting long shadows across the remnants of The Colonel's compound. The once vibrant colors of the island had turned muted and cold, reflecting the grim reality Jack Kincaid now faced. Having defeated The Colonel in a brutal, high-stakes battle, Jack stood over the body of his nemesis, but the victory felt hollow. The Colonel's final words echoed in Jack's mind, and as the sun dipped below the horizon, Jack knew that the fight wasn't truly over.

The scene of their confrontation had been a desperate struggle. The Colonel, though older and scarred, had fought with the ferocity of a man with nothing left to lose. Each blow exchanged between them was laden with years of unresolved anger, guilt, and betrayal. Jack's combat skills, honed through years of service and further sharpened by his time in exile, had finally won out. He had managed to incapacitate The Colonel, but the cost was heavy, and the satisfaction of victory was fleeting.

Jack knelt beside The Colonel's lifeless body, checking for any signs of life, though he knew it was futile. The Colonel's face was twisted in a grimace, his eyes vacant and cold. Jack took a deep breath, his own body aching from the fight. He had won, but it felt like he had lost something far more significant.

Standing up, Jack looked around the compound. The remnants of the smuggling operation were strewn about, evidence of the illicit activities that had plagued the island. Empty crates, broken machinery, and discarded weapons painted a stark picture of the criminal enterprise that had once thrived here. The fire from the earlier battle had left parts of the compound in ruins, and the smoke still lingered in the air.

Jack's thoughts were interrupted by a faint sound coming from inside one of the remaining buildings. Instinctively, he reached for his weapon, his senses alert. Carefully, he approached the building, moving with the precision of a trained operative. The interior was dimly lit, and the air was thick with the smell of smoke and sweat. Jack's heart pounded in his chest as he made his way through the debris.

In a small, makeshift office, Jack found several documents scattered across a desk. They looked like shipping logs and communication records. As he rifled through them, trying to make sense of the scattered papers, he found something that made his blood run cold. There, among the papers, was a list of names and dates that included high-ranking officials—government figures who were clearly involved in The Colonel's operation.

Jack's mind raced. He had suspected that The Colonel's reach extended beyond the island, but seeing concrete evidence of government involvement was a revelation of a different magnitude. The extent of corruption was staggering. These officials were not just passive beneficiaries but active participants in the smuggling ring.

As Jack continued to examine the documents, he discovered a final communication—a plan detailing the evacuation of the remaining supplies and captives. The Colonel had been preparing to flee, but it seemed that Jack had interrupted that process just in time. The plan indicated a rendezvous with a boat that would transport the cargo and people off the island. Jack knew that if he didn't act quickly, more lives could be lost, and the operation could continue elsewhere.

Jack's thoughts were interrupted by the sound of approaching footsteps. He tensed, immediately going into a defensive stance. The door to the office creaked open, and a familiar face emerged from the shadows. It was one of the survivors from earlier, a woman named Elena, who had been particularly vocal about the horrors she had endured.

"Jack," Elena said, her voice trembling. "I was looking for you. I found something that might help."

Jack nodded, motioning for her to follow. Elena handed him a small, encrypted device. "I found this in one of the lockers. I think it might contain important information."

Jack took the device, quickly assessing it. It was a high-tech data storage unit, likely holding crucial intelligence. With a sense of urgency, he hooked it up to his portable system, beginning the process of decrypting its contents.

As the device powered up, Elena watched him with a mixture of hope and fear. "What will happen now?" she asked, her voice tinged with worry.

Jack glanced at her, his face a mask of determination. "I need to find out what's on this device. It might give us a way to expose everything and bring those responsible to justice."

The device beeped, indicating that the decryption was complete. Jack's eyes scanned the screen, and his heart sank as he read through the files. The device contained detailed information about The Colonel's operations, including shipment schedules, contact information for various corrupt officials, and contingency plans for relocating the smuggling network.

But there was something else—an ominous note from The Colonel. It was addressed to his superiors and hinted at a much larger operation, one that extended beyond the island and involved powerful entities at the highest levels of government. The note revealed that The Colonel had been a mere pawn in a much larger scheme. The real masterminds were still out there, pulling the strings and ensuring that the smuggling ring's operations continued smoothly.

Jack felt a wave of frustration and anger. Defeating The Colonel had been a significant victory, but it was clear that the war was far from over. The smuggling ring was only a part of a larger conspiracy, one that reached into the very fabric of government and law enforcement.

Elena's voice broke through his thoughts. "What's next, Jack? What do we do?"

Jack turned to her, his face etched with resolve. "We need to get this information out. The world needs to know what's really going on. But first, we have to ensure that everyone here is safe. We can't let the survivors or the evidence fall into the wrong hands."

Elena nodded, understanding the gravity of the situation. "I'll help you however I can."

Jack quickly formulated a plan. He would contact the outside world, using the encrypted device's information to expose the corruption and dismantle the remaining pieces of the smuggling ring. But he knew that time was running out. The Colonel's allies would soon realize that their operation had been compromised and would be scrambling to cover their tracks.

As Jack prepared to leave the compound, he took one last look at The Colonel's body. The man's death was a step toward justice, but the victory was tainted by the knowledge that the real enemies were still at large. Jack knew that the road ahead would be fraught with danger, but he was determined to see this through. He had already sacrificed too much and lost too many people to back down now.

With Elena's help, Jack began to gather the survivors and organize their evacuation. He knew that they needed to leave the island quickly, but he also needed to ensure that they were safe from any remaining threats. As he worked, he kept a vigilant eye out for any signs of trouble, knowing that the situation could turn dangerous at any moment.

As night fell, Jack and Elena managed to get the survivors to a temporary safe location. Jack contacted a trusted ally who could help them get off the island and into safety. He provided them with the crucial information from the encrypted device, hoping it would be enough to bring the corrupt officials to justice.

With the survivors on their way to safety, Jack took a moment to reflect on the battle he had fought and the hollow victory he had achieved. He had exposed a part of the conspiracy, but the real fight was far from over. As he looked out over the island, he couldn't shake the feeling that the shadows of corruption would continue to loom over him, no matter how far he ran.

Jack knew that the next steps would be dangerous and uncertain, but he was ready to face whatever came his way. The fight against corruption and deception was far from over, and Jack Kincaid was determined to see it through to the end.

Chapter 11: Hunted

The first hint of trouble came in the form of a low, throbbing hum—a sound that didn't belong in Jack Kincaid's carefully curated isolation. He was in the midst of cleaning his weapons, an almost ritualistic activity that calmed him after a long day of skirmishes and strategizing. The weapon in his hands was a finely tuned tool of survival, but as the hum grew louder, Jack knew it wasn't the sound of another motorboat or distant plane. It was the sound of his world being turned upside down.

He stepped out of his makeshift shelter—a converted storage shed fortified with scrap metal and wood—and saw the first of the black SUVs parked at the edge of the dense forest. Their dark, intimidating shapes contrasted sharply with the surrounding greenery. Jack's mind raced, parsing through the possibilities. His immediate thought was that The Colonel's men had returned, but something about this scene felt different. The SUVs were too sophisticated, too clean for the smuggling ring's usual equipment. These were government vehicles, and that meant trouble of a different kind.

Jack's instincts, honed over years of combat and covert operations, told him he had to act fast. He ducked back inside the shelter and grabbed his radio. Static filled the air as he tuned into the frequency he had been using to coordinate with the small group of survivors he had been protecting. He needed to warn them, but there was no guarantee that the interference of government agents wouldn't block the signal.

"Lee, Nora, you there?" Jack's voice crackled through the radio. "We've got incoming. Government vehicles. They're onto us."

There was a moment of silence, then Lee's voice came through, strained and urgent. "We're just getting into position. What's going on?"

Jack's mind raced as he tried to piece together the implications. The government had no reason to come after him unless they were trying to cover their tracks. The only logical conclusion was that he had been framed. His efforts to dismantle The Colonel's operation must have exposed something far more sinister and powerful.

"They're not here for a friendly chat," Jack said grimly. "Get ready to move. We're going to have to figure out how to outsmart these guys and find a way off this island before they catch us."

The radio went silent as Lee and Nora acknowledged his warning and began their preparations. Jack knew their situation was precarious. The Colonel's operation had left a bloody trail, and now Jack was the scapegoat, the perfect cover for those who wished to remain hidden in the shadows.

Jack grabbed his backpack and slung it over his shoulder. Inside were critical supplies: food, water, ammunition, and a few personal mementos that reminded him of why he was fighting. He grabbed a set of night-vision goggles and slung a silenced weapon across his back. He needed to stay hidden and get out of sight before the government agents began their sweep.

He approached the edge of the forest, moving cautiously to avoid detection. The dense foliage provided some cover, but he knew that it wouldn't be enough if they were actively searching for him. As he neared a vantage point, he saw the first of the agents disembarking from the SUVs. They were methodical, professional—evidence that these weren't ordinary government operatives. Their movements suggested training and experience, likely from elite units accustomed to handling high-stakes operations.

Jack's heart pounded as he scanned the area. His tactical mind analyzed their formation, noting the locations of vehicles and the patterns of their patrols. He needed to gather more information before making any moves. He could see a few agents setting up a temporary command post near the edge of the forest, their activity punctuated by the occasional flash of a camera or the click of a radio.

As he observed, Jack noticed something that made his blood run cold. A figure, standing apart from the rest, was observing the area with an unsettling calmness. The man was tall, with a military bearing and an air of authority that spoke volumes. He wore a dark suit, sharply tailored, and his presence commanded immediate attention. This was no ordinary field operative; this was someone with a significant role in this operation.

Jack's instincts flared. The man's posture and the way he surveyed the surroundings suggested he was the orchestrator behind this entire setup. If Jack was going to get out of this alive, he would need to confront this individual directly. The question was how to get close without being caught.

With calculated movements, Jack made his way towards the command post, staying in the shadows and using the dense vegetation to his advantage. He could hear snippets of conversation—agents discussing their next moves, talking about a high-profile case involving Jack Kincaid, and the urgency of their mission. The mention of his name confirmed his fears. They were here to pin the smuggling ring's crimes on him.

He reached a position close enough to overhear more details. The agents were preparing to raid his hideout. They were going to search it thoroughly and gather evidence that would link him to The Colonel's operations. Jack needed to act fast. He couldn't afford to let them find anything that could incriminate him.

Jack carefully retreated from the area, moving back towards his shelter. His mind was racing with strategies. He had to find Lee and Nora, get them to safety, and figure out a way to clear his name. But with government agents closing in, every minute counted.

As he approached his shelter, he found Lee and Nora already there, ready and waiting. Lee's face was set in determination, while Nora looked anxious but resolute.

"They're planning to raid our hideout," Jack said urgently. "We need to move now, before they get their hands on anything that could implicate us."

The trio quickly packed up their supplies, making sure to leave behind anything that could be linked to their presence. Jack's mind was consumed with a single thought: he needed to find the man in the dark suit—the one who was orchestrating this entire setup. This was the key to proving his innocence or at least finding a way to turn the tide in his favor.

"Where do we go?" Nora asked as they prepared to leave.

Jack scanned the surrounding forest. "We'll head to the northern part of the island. It's less accessible, and we can use the terrain to our advantage. We need to stay off their radar until we figure out our next move."

As they set off, Jack's thoughts were consumed by the gravity of their situation. The government was framing him, and they had the resources and power to make it stick. His days of being a lone wolf were over. He needed allies, and he needed them fast. But with the threat of being captured or worse hanging over him, trust was a luxury he couldn't afford.

They moved silently through the forest, each step calculated and deliberate. The sounds of their environment—distant waves crashing against the shore, the rustle of leaves in the wind—were both a comfort and a reminder of their precarious situation. Jack's senses were on high alert, every noise and shadow analyzed for potential threats.

As they neared the northern part of the island, Jack's thoughts turned to the figure in the dark suit. Who was he, and what was his role in this elaborate scheme? Jack knew that uncovering the truth behind this man was essential to clearing his name and dismantling the corruption that had ensnared him.

The sun began to set, casting long shadows across the forest floor. Jack knew that the darkness would provide some cover, but it also meant that they had to be even more cautious. They set up a temporary camp in a secluded area, hidden from prying eyes. Jack took the first watch, his mind racing with plans and possibilities.

As the night deepened, Jack's thoughts turned to his past—the mission that had gone wrong, the betrayal, and the long road to redemption. He had always believed that he could escape his past by living in isolation, but the harsh reality was that it had followed him here. Now, more than ever, he needed to confront it and find a way to emerge victorious.

The distant sound of footsteps and the occasional crackle of radio chatter reminded him that they were not alone. Jack's resolve hardened. He would find the man in the dark suit, expose the conspiracy, and clear his name. It was no longer just about survival; it was about justice and redemption.

As the first light of dawn began to filter through the trees, Jack prepared himself for the challenges ahead. The government's net was tightening around him, and the stakes had never been higher. But Jack Kincaid was a man who thrived under pressure. He had faced countless adversaries, and now, he was ready to face the ultimate challenge: the powerful forces that had conspired to frame him for crimes he didn't commit.

The battle for his freedom was just beginning, and Jack Kincaid was determined to fight until the very end.

Jack Kincaid's world had spiraled into a violent blur, one he hadn't been able to escape from. The Colonel's death had not marked the end of his torment but merely the beginning of a more insidious nightmare. With the Colonel's allies in the government working tirelessly to cover their tracks, Jack now found himself framed for crimes he had fought so hard to thwart.

The island was no longer a sanctuary but a trap. As he moved through the dense jungle, the familiar sounds of the forest had become distorted, every rustle and snap of a twig twisting into the ominous echoes of pursuers closing in. The sense of isolation that once provided him solace now seemed like a cruel joke. The silent, imposing landscape was filled with the ghosts of his past and the reality of his current predicament.

Jack had been working through the night, hiding evidence, and trying to piece together any semblance of a plan. He knew that whoever had orchestrated this frame-up was thorough and powerful, with the resources to reach even the most remote corners of the globe. He needed to think fast. There was no room for error, no margin for miscalculation.

He had managed to stay one step ahead of the initial wave of government agents sent to capture him, but he knew that their numbers were growing, and their determination unwavering. The weight of his situation settled heavily on his shoulders as he crouched beneath a canopy of tangled vines, listening to the hum of helicopters overhead and the distant crackle of radios.

Jack's thoughts raced as he calculated his next move. The evidence against him was overwhelming: weapons, drugs, and even a ledger detailing transactions that linked him to the smuggling ring. Each piece of fabricated evidence had been meticulously planted, leaving no room for plausible deniability. He had to clear his name, but how could he when he was being hunted by those who controlled the narrative?

His attention was drawn to a rustling noise nearby. He instinctively reached for his weapon, but it was only a small animal skittering through the underbrush. Jack exhaled slowly, his pulse steadying. The presence of the animal was a reminder of how isolated he truly was, how the island, once a symbol of his self-imposed exile, had become a battleground.

Jack's thoughts returned to his few remaining allies—if they could still be called that. Their loyalty was fragile at best, tested by fear and self-preservation. Jack had to assume that the government's influence had reached them as well, making trust a luxury he could no longer afford.

As the first light of dawn began to break through the dense foliage, Jack knew he needed to find a way off the island. He had two options: secure a boat and head for open water or find a way to contact someone who could provide him with the evidence to expose the truth. The former seemed more plausible given the urgency of his situation. The island's only boat, an old and unreliable vessel, was hidden in a secluded cove—a place he hadn't visited in weeks.

Jack navigated through the forest with the precision of a man who had spent years in such conditions. Each step was calculated, every sound analyzed. He moved quickly but quietly, his training guiding him through the labyrinthine trails of the jungle. He reached the cove just as the sun was climbing higher in the sky, casting long shadows over the rocky shore.

The boat was still where he had left it, though it had seen better days. Jack examined it carefully, checking for any signs of tampering. The engine was old, and the fuel was likely stale, but it was functional. With a mixture of relief and trepidation, Jack began the task of preparing the boat for departure.

As he worked, Jack couldn't shake the feeling of being watched. Every now and then, he'd catch a fleeting glimpse of movement in the trees or hear a distant sound that set his instincts on high alert. The sense of being constantly observed heightened his anxiety but also sharpened his focus. He knew he had to complete his preparations and leave before the government agents closed in on him again.

It took hours to get the boat ready. Jack had just finished securing the last of the supplies when he heard the unmistakable sound of approaching vehicles. Panic surged through him. There was no time to lose. He hastily untied the boat and pushed it into the water, climbing aboard with the practiced ease of someone who had spent more time on boats than on dry land.

As the boat eased away from the shore, Jack glanced back at the island. It seemed peaceful and serene, a stark contrast to the chaos that had unfolded. He felt a pang of regret for the life he was leaving behind, but there was no turning back now. The open sea lay ahead, and with it, the hope of escape.

Jack steered the boat toward the horizon, his mind racing with the enormity of his situation. He was now a fugitive, hunted by the very government he had once served. The sense of betrayal was overwhelming. The people he had trusted, the institutions he had believed in, had all turned against him.

The ocean was vast and unforgiving. Jack had always felt a deep connection to the sea, but now it felt like an endless expanse of uncertainty. He had no clear destination, no map to guide him, only the distant hope that he could find refuge somewhere beyond the reach of his pursuers.

Hours turned into days as Jack navigated the open waters, surviving on the limited supplies he had managed to bring with him. The days were spent scanning the horizon for any sign of land or pursuing vessels, while the nights were filled with restless thoughts and the haunting memories of his past.

His mind kept returning to the evidence he had discovered: the documents, the ledger, and the incriminating files that linked the powerful figures in the government to the smuggling ring. Jack knew that if he could get this evidence to the right people, he might be able to clear his name and expose the corruption. But getting the evidence to the public would be a challenge in itself, especially with the government's reach extending into every corner of the globe.

As the days wore on, Jack's hope began to wane. The ocean seemed to stretch on forever, and the isolation was beginning to take its toll. He was exhausted, both physically and mentally. The constant vigilance, the fear of being discovered, and the uncertainty of his situation had left him worn thin.

One evening, as Jack scanned the horizon once more, he spotted a faint outline of land in the distance. It was a small island, much like the one he had left behind. Relief surged through him as he adjusted the boat's course, making his way toward the island. It was a risky move, but it was better than drifting aimlessly in the open sea.

As he approached the island, Jack's senses were on high alert. He knew that any sign of activity could mean trouble. The small island seemed deserted, with no signs of life or civilization. Jack docked the boat and made his way ashore, cautiously exploring the area for any signs of danger.

The island was small and barren, with little to offer in terms of resources. Jack set up a makeshift camp and began to assess his situation. He needed to find a way to get the evidence to the outside world, but without access to communication or reliable transportation, his options were limited.

As he sat by the campfire, Jack thought about his next steps. He knew that he couldn't stay on the island for long. The government's reach was extensive, and it was only a matter of time before they found him. He needed to come up with a plan to get the evidence to someone who could help him, someone who could expose the truth.

In the silence of the night, Jack's thoughts turned to his past and the choices he had made. He had always been a man of action, but now he found himself in a position where his actions seemed futile. He wondered if there was a way to turn the tide, to fight back against the forces that had turned his life upside down.

As dawn approached, Jack resolved to take action. He would find a way to get the evidence out of his possession and into the hands of those who could use it to expose the corruption. The small island might not offer much in terms of resources, but it provided him with the opportunity to regroup and plan his next move.

With renewed determination, Jack set about preparing for his departure. He knew that the journey ahead would be dangerous and uncertain, but he was prepared to face whatever challenges lay ahead. The open sea awaited, and with it, the chance to clear his name and fight back against those who had betrayed him.

As he made his final preparations, Jack took one last look at the small island. It was a place of refuge and solace, but it was also a reminder of the challenges he faced. With a deep breath and a resolute heart, Jack set sail once more, ready to face the unknown and fight for his freedom.

Chapter 12: Into the Deep

Jack Kincaid stood alone at the edge of the dense jungle, his face shadowed under the brim of a battered baseball cap. The moonlight filtered through the thick canopy above, casting a ghostly pallor over the island's rugged landscape. It had been days since he'd lost contact with the survivors he'd vowed to protect, and now he was certain they were all gone. The realization hit him hard, like a punch to the gut, but he had no time to mourn. His entire world had collapsed around him, and survival was all that mattered.

His once-trusted allies had turned on him, and the betrayal stung more than any physical wound. The survivors had been his only connection to hope, and now, stripped of their support, he was a man without a base, a shadow in the night. His instincts screamed that the enemy was closing in, and he had to move. But where to?

Jack had spent the past few hours scouring the jungle for any trace of the surviving mercenaries or government agents who might have been sent to hunt him down. The jungle was eerily quiet, save for the occasional rustle of leaves and the distant calls of nocturnal creatures. He was acutely aware of the irony: this place, which had once been his sanctuary, had now become a prison.

The betrayal had come swiftly and without warning. Just a few nights earlier, he had discovered that the allies he'd relied on had been compromised. The Colonel's powerful connections had managed to corrupt the small circle of trust he'd built. Their turncoat actions had led to the capture or death of most of the survivors, and the island's security had been breached.

Jack had overheard a conversation—snatched through the crackling interference of a makeshift radio he had managed to intercept. The voices were muffled and distorted, but the intent was clear: his remaining allies had been coerced or bribed to turn against him. The betrayal wasn't merely a personal attack; it was a systematic dismantling of the last vestiges of his resistance.

In the dead of night, he had watched from the shadows as his erstwhile comrades, now agents of the conspiracy, led a group of heavily armed men through the dense foliage. They moved with purpose and precision, betraying an intimate knowledge of the island's hidden pathways. Jack had managed to evade detection, but the sight of his allies working against him had been a bitter pill to swallow.

With the island's defenses compromised, Jack had no choice but to go on the run. The tactical advantage he had once enjoyed was slipping away, replaced by a dangerous game of cat and mouse. His every move was now shadowed by unseen enemies, and he had to rely on his survival skills and the element of surprise.

The first order of business was to get off the island. But escaping was no easy feat. The Colonel's influence reached deep into the heart of the government, and the island was crawling with operatives who would stop at nothing to capture or kill him. The small boat he had used to patrol the island was long gone, seized by his betrayers, leaving him with limited options.

He navigated through the jungle with the careful precision of a seasoned operative, utilizing every ounce of his training. His mind was a whirlwind of tactical calculations and strategic plans, each step meticulously calculated to avoid detection. His instincts, honed by years of military service, guided him through the labyrinthine terrain.

Jack made his way to the island's northern coast, where he knew the rough waters and treacherous currents made it less accessible. The harsh conditions would have been a deterrent for most, but for Jack, they were an advantage. The rough seas would help cover his escape, provided he could find a way to get to the water.

He stumbled upon a small, dilapidated dock, barely visible through the undergrowth. The wooden planks were rotting and half-submerged, but it was his best option. A quick inspection revealed a small, rusted boat tethered to the dock. It wasn't much, but it was seaworthy enough to get him off the island.

Jack approached the boat cautiously, scanning the surroundings for any sign of movement. The last thing he needed was to be caught while preparing his escape. The boat was a relic of the island's past, but Jack knew he could make it work. He untied the rope, shoved the boat into the water, and climbed aboard.

The engine roared to life with a sputter and a cough, but it held steady. Jack navigated the boat away from the dock, the small vessel bobbing unsteadily in the rough waters. The island receded into the distance, its dark silhouette swallowed by the night. As he steered towards the open ocean, Jack knew that he was leaving behind a place that had once been his refuge, now a symbol of his greatest defeat.

He set a course for the nearest shipping lanes, hoping to find a vessel that could take him to safety. The ocean was a vast and unpredictable expanse, but it offered anonymity, a chance to disappear from the radar of his pursuers.

As the boat surged through the waves, Jack's thoughts turned to the survivors he had failed to protect. The weight of their loss was a heavy burden, one he would carry with him into the unknown. The stakes had never been higher, and the cost of failure was now measured in lives lost and trust betrayed.

Jack's mind raced through the next steps of his plan. He needed to find a way to clear his name, but with the government's machinations against him, that would be nearly impossible. His only chance was to uncover the full extent of the conspiracy and expose the powerful figures behind it.

The boat chugged along, and the night wore on. The horizon remained a dark, unbroken line, offering no solace. Jack knew he was a hunted man, his former life a distant memory. The ghosts of his past, the failure that had driven him into exile, now seemed to be closing in on him with a vengeance.

He could see the faint lights of a distant cargo ship, a beacon of hope in the vast darkness. Jack's heart raced as he maneuvered the boat towards the vessel, desperate for a chance to board and find refuge. The ship's lights grew brighter, and Jack readied himself for the next phase of his desperate escape.

The cargo ship loomed larger, its massive hull cutting through the water. Jack maneuvered the boat alongside it, using a rope to climb aboard. He scanned the deck for any signs of activity, his senses on high alert. The ship was eerily quiet, the only sound the lapping of the waves against the hull.

Jack crept across the deck, careful to avoid detection. His instincts told him that this was a risky move, but it was his best option for now. He needed to find a way to blend in, to disappear into the crowd of the ship's crew. As he approached the bridge, he could hear the low murmur of voices. The crew was on watch, their conversation punctuated by occasional bursts of laughter.

Jack ducked into the shadows, waiting for the right moment to slip inside. His mind was a whirl of strategy and caution, every movement calculated to avoid detection. He had to remain hidden until he could figure out his next move.

As he settled into a small, dark corner of the ship, Jack took a deep breath and tried to steady his racing thoughts. The ocean was his only sanctuary now, a place where he could regroup and plan his next move. But the threat of being discovered was ever-present, and he knew that his time was running out.

The ship's engines roared as it picked up speed, and Jack felt a sense of fleeting relief. He was no longer on the island, but the battle was far from over. The conspiracy he faced was vast and insidious, and the ghosts of his past were ever-present.

Jack closed his eyes and tried to focus on the task at hand. He needed to stay hidden, to find a way to expose the conspiracy and clear his name. But with powerful enemies closing in, the odds were stacked against him. The open sea was his refuge, but it was also a reminder of how far he had fallen.

As the ship sailed further into the night, Jack resolved to use every ounce of his training and resourcefulness to survive. The fight was not over, and he would not give up. The road ahead was fraught with danger, but Jack Kincaid was determined to see it through to the end.

With the ship's lights fading into the distance, Jack knew that his journey was far from over. The open ocean stretched out before him, a vast and unforgiving expanse. But for Jack, it was a place of both peril and possibility, a chance to reclaim his life and seek justice for those he had lost. The battle against his own demons was just beginning, and he was ready to face whatever lay ahead.

The wind howled across the island, whipping through the broken trees and stirring the waves to a frenzy. Jack Kincaid stood at the edge of the rocky shore, staring out at the vast expanse of water that lay before him. The island, once his refuge from the world, had become his prison. Now, it was the only thing standing between him and an uncertain future.

The small boat he had managed to commandeer bobbed up and down in the turbulent surf, barely visible in the dim light of the fading day. Jack had stripped it of anything unnecessary, making it as light and fast as possible. The smuggling ring was dismantled, and The Colonel was dead, but his victory was hollow. The power behind the operation—the government figures who had funded and protected The Colonel's empire—had turned their sights on him. Jack was now a fugitive, framed for the very crimes he had fought to stop.

His body ached from the relentless fighting, every muscle sore from the countless skirmishes and narrow escapes. Blood still trickled from a fresh cut above his brow, a reminder of how close he had come to losing everything. But this wasn't the end—not yet. There was still one fight left, and it wasn't one Jack could win with fists or bullets. It was a battle for survival, one that would take him far from the island that had once been his sanctuary.

He glanced back toward the dense trees, knowing that the few allies he had left had either fled or turned against him. Betrayal had become a constant companion, and Jack could no longer afford to trust anyone. The last woman he had saved, Maria, had looked at him with the same eyes that once pleaded for help, but now there was fear. Fear of what he had become. She had left with the others, disappearing into the jungle, leaving him alone.

The rumble of distant engines pulled Jack from his thoughts. He knew the sound well—government agents, closing in. They were methodical, sweeping the island in grid patterns, searching for any sign of him. They wouldn't stop until they found him, and when they did, Jack knew there would be no trial, no opportunity to clear his name. They would kill him on sight.

Jack took a deep breath, the salty air filling his lungs. There was no more time to linger. He checked the supplies on his boat—just enough food and water to last a few days, maybe more if he rationed carefully. His destination wasn't clear, but he had no intention of staying put. He had to keep moving, to disappear into the vastness of the Pacific.

His thoughts drifted back to the woman who had washed ashore, her story igniting the fire in him once again. The trafficked women had all been sent off to safety, the operation dismantled, but their suffering had been a grim reminder of the evils lurking in the shadows. Jack had made a difference, but the price was steep. He wasn't a hero in the eyes of the world. He was a ghost now, a hunted man with no place to call home.

The boat rocked beneath him as he climbed aboard, pushing off from the shore. The engine sputtered to life, the roar swallowed by the crashing waves. Jack guided the vessel through the rough waters, his hands steady on the wheel despite the storm brewing around him. The island grew smaller in the distance, fading into the mist until it was just a dark smudge on the horizon.

As the hours passed, the adrenaline that had kept him moving began to fade, leaving him with nothing but the weight of his thoughts. The Colonel's face haunted him, not because of the man's betrayal, but because of the truth he had revealed in their final moments. The Colonel had been a pawn, just like Jack. Used, discarded, and betrayed by the very system they had sworn to protect. It was a bitter irony that the mission that had destroyed Jack's life had been part of a larger conspiracy, one that had claimed the lives of innocent civilians for profit and power.

The Colonel had known too much, and now, so did Jack. That's why they wanted him dead. He was the last loose end in a web of lies that stretched far beyond the island, far beyond the smugglers, the mercenaries, or the traffickers. Jack didn't have all the pieces yet, but he knew enough to be dangerous. And that made him a target.

The open sea stretched out in every direction, a vast, endless void that mirrored the emptiness Jack felt inside. He had once been part of something greater—a Navy SEAL, a protector of freedom. But now, all he had was this boat and the ghosts of his past. The people he had lost, the men and women who had died because of decisions he had made—they were all still with him, their faces flickering in his mind like shadows.

A flash of lightning lit up the sky, and Jack squinted against the brightness. The storm was closing in, and with it came the promise of even rougher seas. He'd faced worse, but out here, alone in the ocean, there were no allies to call for backup, no base to retreat to. It was just him, the storm, and whatever lay beyond.

The boat creaked under the strain of the rising waves, each one threatening to capsize it. Jack braced himself, steering the vessel into the swells, riding the crests and navigating the valleys of water that seemed to come from every direction. His hands gripped the wheel tightly, muscles straining as he fought to keep control.

Hours passed, though it felt like days. The storm raged on, but Jack didn't waver. He was used to being in the thick of the fight, used to facing down insurmountable odds. The only difference now was that there was no one left to fight beside him. No team, no mission, just survival. And survival, Jack reminded himself, was something he had mastered long ago.

As the night dragged on, Jack found himself thinking about the future—if he even had one. He could disappear, fade into the backdrop of some forgotten corner of the world, living out his days in anonymity. Or he could go back, take the fight to those who had framed him, expose the truth, and clear his name. But that path seemed more dangerous than anything he'd ever faced. Powerful people wanted him silenced, and they had the means to do it.

The boat lurched suddenly, a massive wave crashing over the bow and soaking Jack to the bone. He cursed under his breath, adjusting the course as best he could. The storm showed no signs of letting up, and exhaustion was beginning to take its toll. Every muscle in his body screamed for rest, but Jack knew he couldn't afford to stop. Not yet.

As dawn broke, the storm finally began to abate, the angry clouds giving way to a dim, gray sky. The sea, though still rough, had calmed enough for Jack to finally catch his breath. He sat back, letting the engine idle as the boat drifted. For the first time in what felt like days, he allowed himself to close his eyes, if only for a moment.

But even as he rested, his mind raced. The Colonel's death had left a void, but the machine behind the smuggling ring would continue to operate, driven by greed and corruption. Jack knew that if he wanted to stop it, he would have to find the ones pulling the strings—the men in suits, the politicians, the shadowy figures hiding behind government walls. And that meant going back into the world he had tried so hard to leave behind.

The sun crept higher in the sky, casting a pale light over the water. Jack opened his eyes, staring at the horizon. The island was long gone, but the memories remained, burned into his mind like scars that would never fully heal.

With a deep breath, Jack reached for the throttle, guiding the boat toward an uncertain future. He didn't know where he was headed, but one thing was clear: the fight wasn't over. It would never be over. Not for someone like him.

The engine roared to life, and the boat surged forward, cutting through the waves with purpose. Jack Kincaid was many things—soldier, killer, survivor. But above all, he was a man who couldn't let go of the past, no matter how far he ran.

As the coastline disappeared behind him, Jack kept his eyes on the horizon, the vast ocean stretching out before him like an open wound. Somewhere out there, his enemies were waiting. But Jack wasn't afraid. He had faced death before, and he would face it again.

Because in the end, Jack Kincaid wasn't running from his past.

He was running toward it.

And this time, he wouldn't stop until every last secret was brought to light.

As the boat sailed into the unknown, Jack allowed himself a small, bitter smile. The tides of deception had carried him this far, but now it was his turn to chart the course.

And wherever it led, Jack knew one thing for certain:

He was ready.

Don't miss out!

Visit the website below and you can sign up to receive emails whenever Michael Ferguson publishes a new book. There's no charge and no obligation.

https://books2read.com/r/B-A-CKNW-XADAF

BOOKS 2 READ

Connecting independent readers to independent writers.

Did you love *Tides Of Deception*? Then you should read *Ink and Blood*[1] by Michael Ferguson!

[2]

Journalist Daniel Harper has built his career exposing the darkest corners of corruption and uncovering untold truths. But nothing could prepare him for his latest investigation—a series of brutal murders gripping the city, each one chillingly similar to the scenes from a popular horror series by the reclusive novelist Sebastian Vale. At first, Daniel dismisses the connection as a morbid coincidence. However, as more bodies surface, the similarities between fiction and reality become impossible to ignore.

---

1. https://books2read.com/u/47Bzxj

2. https://books2read.com/u/47Bzxj

Obsessed with uncovering the truth, Daniel dives deep into the life of Sebastian Vale, a mysterious figure whose books seem to predict real-life events down to their grisliest details. But this time, the scenes Vale writes haven't been published yet, and the murders keep following his yet-to-be-released work. Daniel's investigation quickly turns personal as he begins receiving anonymous tips, finding cryptic clues, and sensing an invisible hand guiding his every move. The deeper he digs, the more Daniel's sense of control slips away.

Then comes a horrifying revelation: Sebastian Vale has the ability to bring his stories to life, and Daniel is the protagonist in his latest twisted narrative. Every move Daniel makes, every discovery, every conversation is part of Vale's unfolding script. Worse still, the manuscript details a grisly fate for Daniel—his own murder, already written, already destined to occur.

As Daniel spirals into paranoia and dread, his relationships fracture and his career teeters on the brink. The boundaries between fiction and reality blur beyond recognition, and Daniel begins questioning the very fabric of his existence. Could his entire life have been a story written by Vale? Is he merely a character in someone else's tale, devoid of free will, living out a narrative that was planned from the beginning?

In a race against time, Daniel embarks on a desperate mission to stop Vale and rewrite his fate. But the final chapters of Vale's manuscript reveal a truth more horrifying than anything Daniel could have imagined: his death has already occurred. His life, his investigation, his memories—all are part of a novel that has already reached its tragic conclusion. Daniel was never truly alive. He was always just ink and blood on the pages of a book.

With his fate sealed in words, Daniel must confront the terrifying realization that his story—like the lives of the other victims—was never his own. As the clock ticks down to his final moments, he faces an inescapable truth: he can't outrun the narrative that has already been written. The only question that remains is, how will it end?

Ink and Blood is a psychological thriller that blurs the lines between fiction and reality, where the protagonist's life is controlled by the power of the written word. In this chilling tale, readers will be gripped by the suspense as Daniel Harper unravels a mystery that leaves him questioning not only the world around him but also his very existence. From intricate twists to shocking revelations, Ink and Blood will keep you on the edge of your seat until its tragic, unforgettable conclusion.